THE LAST CHANCE

C A F É

AND OTHER STORIES

THE LAST CHANCE
CAFÉ
AND OTHER STORIES

ANITA ROBERTS

POLESTAR
BOOK PUBLISHERS

The Last Chance Café

Published by:
Polestar Press Ltd.
6496 Youngs North Road
Winlaw, B.C., V0G 2J0
and
2758 Charles Street
Vancouver, B.C., V5K 3A7

The publisher gratefully acknowledges the financial support of
The Canada Council, The Department of Communications,
and The British Columbia Cultural Services Branch.

Earlier versions of some of these stories have appeared in:
Other Voices, *Prism International*, **Catholic Girls** (Penguin),
The Dark Side of Love (Crossing Press),
and *The Texas Journal of Women and the Law*.

Editing by Suzanne Bastedo.
Author photograph and cover photograph by Jamie Griffiths.
Photo tinting and cover design by Jim Brennan.
Interior illustrations by Mia Tremblay.
Production by Michelle Benjamin.
Printed in Canada on recycled paper by Best-Gagne.

Canadian Cataloguing in Publication Data
Roberts, Anita, 1952-
        The last chance café
ISBN   0-919591-80-9
I. Title.
PS8585.0247L3 1993   C813'.54   C93-091690-5
PR9199.3.R624L3 1993

Special thanks to:

Mildred Tremblay, Betsy Warland and Daphne Marlatt for opening doorways; Maggie Zeigler, Adrianne Ross and Frances Ross for helping me to examine the doors; Betty Baxter for showing me there was no ceiling and being the safe room on the other side for so long; Sara, Louise and Paula for "seeing" me and "taking me home";

and Mia Tremblay for her gentle nudges off the pedestal and her beautiful drawings;

and my editor, Suzanne Bastedo, for entering my body of work with such sensitivity and precision;

and my cousin Deb and my friend Laurie who accompany me on my quest for the Princess Poison Antidote;

and Michelle Benjamin, my publisher: thank you for this act of faith.

The Last Chance Café
and other stories

Through the first doorway of my mother's body, through that first dark terror into the opening that she made for me, it hurt to see, but I learned and I continued on my journey. I have learned not to run screaming down dark hallways, crashing through doorways into the rooms of pain exploding in my face like a fist. Each time, in the end, finding myself outside the same door, bruised and broken.

I have learned to accept the dark, examine the doorways. They are my teachers now.

The Last Chance Café

For all my sisters

ANNA AND HER SISTERS lived in the back of the Last Chance Café. The café, with general store and gas station, was fifty miles south of the next small town on the highway. Last chance to eat and gas up before heading north. Last chance to have a happy childhood.

The house was just a couple of rooms built onto the back of the store. Anna slept with her five sisters in a long room, the narrow cast-iron beds all side by side. Six girls, no boys. Anna was the third girl not born a boy.

Anna usually woke up Sunday mornings with a little bird of anxiety stirring in her tummy. Church day. It wasn't that Anna didn't like church. She liked the singing and the Latin phrases she had memorized until she knew them all by heart: "*Agnus De-e-i, Qui tollis peccata mundi, Miserari no-o-bis...*" She had no idea what the phrases meant but that didn't matter. They were like one long exotic word to her.

The little bird whispered, "Get up! Get up!" Anna sat up and looked over at the bed beside hers, at the mound that was her oldest sister, Theresa. Theresa had chosen Anna as her room-mate after the partition had gone up. Now that there were two rooms, Theresa and Anna were sharing the smaller one; that meant Anna was *in* right now. Being *in* with Theresa meant being allowed to try on her nylons. And it meant Theresa would put Anna's hair up in a bun and apply copious amounts of makeup to Anna's eyes and lips all the while telling her juicy stories about sex and boys. Anna didn't recall doing anything to deserve this special privilege and wasn't even sure if she actually enjoyed it, but she knew it made her other sisters envious and that was definitely a plus.

The little bird in Anna's tummy flexed its wings and stretched its neck nervously. Anna started dressing for church. She rummaged through the pile of clothes on the floor near her bed and chose a cotton dress that wasn't too badly wrinkled. It wasn't cotton dress weather but that wasn't something anyone in her family ever considered.

She walked sleepily into the other room and started

digging through the socks and underwear drawers for a matching pair of something. Most of the family's clothes were kept in an enormous nine-drawer dresser in the big room that her other four sisters shared. The dresser always had its nine drawers open like enormous mouths regurgitating articles of clothing and spewing out underwear and socks which dribbled in bits and holey pieces onto the floor. Inevitably, a stray would be kicked under a bed to be lost among the clouds of dust collected there. A matched pair of anything was a rare find.

This particular morning, Anna did find two white bobby socks that looked enough like a pair. The hole in one heel wouldn't show if she scrunched the sock down far enough under her foot. This created an uncomfortable bulge, but she decided it wouldn't be unbearable because she knew she would spend a lot of the time in church on her knees.

As she observed the unmoving lumps of blankets on her sisters' beds, the little bird fluttered in her chest again. "C'mon, you guys…get up!" she hissed between her teeth.

Anna saw Toni sit up and could hear Theresa stretching and yawning languorously in the other room. Lou just pulled the covers over her head. She hated to get out of bed in the morning.

"You're gonna get it!" Anna warned, and then she heard her father's footsteps approaching the door. A wild flapping started in that space just between her ribs, that little triangle spot that made her feel sick if she pressed it too hard. Anna ran quickly into the bathroom and locked the door. She stood in front of the mirror and stared at her face. Soft brown eyes, soft brown hair waving down to her shoulders, soft brown freckles sprinkled over her nose. She stood very, very still; she was listening with her whole body.

"What? Not up yet, eh?" Her dad's voice. The cold steel one. Then a crying out and Anna could see, as though reflected in the mirror before her, Lou desperately hanging onto the covers in a futile attempt to protect her brand-new breasts from his hungry eyes. Anna cringed with the shame that she knew Lou felt.

"Dad, please...no...Dad, please don't!" Lou's pathetic cries pierced Anna's skin. She closed her eyes tight and clenched her fists.

"Get up, you lazy bum!"

Anna's cheeks flushed hot as she heard the loud smack and Lou's ensuing howl. "Oh no," she prayed, "don't scream like that—he'll only hit you more! Oh God, please make Lou stop screaming." But she knew it was no use. She sat down on the toilet lid and stared at the floor.

"Stop your bloody screaming, you big baby! You think you have something to scream about? I'll give you something to scream about! Shut up, you little bitch...I said, SHUT UP!"

"*Ow, Ow, Ow!* My hair, my hair! Dad, it *hurts!*"

Anna's scalp tingled and Lou's screams got louder. They were edged with panic now.

"Hysterical little bitch! Shut up right now or you'll be really sorry...I said, NOW!"

The screaming stopped suddenly and was replaced by choking and gagging sounds, desperate sounds that washed over Anna as she sat, slumped over, her knees apart and her hands lying numbly in her lap.

The numbness began to spread like an anaesthetic throughout her whole body. The sounds from the next room began to thin so that she heard them as though from a great distance. As she sat staring at the bathroom floor, whorls of white on the green tiles caught her eye. On the corner of one tile there was a kind of face and she studied it in earnest, fleshing it out. White smears of eyes with an Olive Oyl cartoon nose and a grin that got carried away, sweeping right out the side of the face. As her eyes followed the wild end of the grin, up and around, it became the tail of a three-legged dog and soon she found a bird and a fish—no, a shark. She pulled her eyes quickly away, then went back in search of the face. At first she couldn't find it at all and then there it was gazing at her blankly. She gazed blankly back.

A hiccupping sob came from the other room. She stepped softly to the bathroom door to listen. He was gone.

Lou was two years older, but Anna didn't follow her example when it came to dealing with her dad. Lou was always *getting it.* So was Theresa. Anna watched them both carefully and knew exactly what not to do. She thought they must be stupid. It seemed as though they were almost asking for it. Couldn't they see?

Anna emerged from the bathroom with both hands cupped over her tummy to still the fluttering that had started up again. She didn't look at Lou as she walked by to get her shoes. She strapped them on. They were hand-me-down Mary Janes and they were too small. This, like the sock, didn't matter. She was just glad they weren't brown oxfords like the ones her dad had just bought for Lou and Theresa. Boys' shoes. She rubbed her palm over the shiny black surfaces of her Mary Janes and, pressing firmly with her index finger, stuck down a piece of the vinyl that had begun to peel up.

To reach the laundry room and find a cardigan, she must once more walk by Lou. This time she glanced sidelong and saw that Lou had begun to dress. Relief. As Lou pulled on a corduroy jumper, she gulped air in short spasms through her mouth, causing her bottom lip to suck in over her teeth. Feeling-sorry-for-yourself sounds, thought Anna.

In the laundry room, Anna ploughed through a mountain of clothes—the clean pile—and pulled out a sweater. One button was missing and two of the others were dangling by threads, but the blue of the sweater matched her dress, so she put it on. The sock with the hole had wriggled its way under her heel. When she bent down to pull the sock up, she saw two chubby feet in the open crack of the cupboard door. One small foot was folded protectively over the other and the toes were scrunched up tight.

"Suzie?" Anna slid the door open and saw her four-year-old sister curled up, arms wrapped around her knees. Suzie looked up at her big sister with round eyes.

"Hey, silly!" Anna said. "What are you doing in there? C'mon, you have to get dressed for church!"

Suzie didn't answer, but allowed Anna to help her out of the cupboard. She was silent as Anna handed her an assortment of clothes to put on. Suzie was always the quiet one.

"I was being invisible," she said.

Anna made her way through the back door onto the boardwalk that ran between the house and the store and through another door into the back room. The back room was a small storage area nestled between the kitchen of the café and Anna's parents' bedroom. She could hear muffled arguing coming from behind their door as she slipped silently by.

Anna lingered for a moment, smelling the kitchen smells of french fries and cold hamburger grease and feeling her hunger, which was somehow always more intense on Sunday mornings. She knew better than to eat before church, though, and resisted even the small temptation of dipping her finger into the big tub of butter as she walked by. As she looked at the clean-scraped grill, the thought of the porous cleaning stone sliding over it made her shiver a nails-on-the-blackboard kind of shiver.

She wove her way around to the front of the store, past the long coffee counter, and then stopped at the candy bar stand. She inhaled deeply the amalgam of waxed paper and chocolate. Sweet Marie and Oh Henry. She imagined them as girlfriend and boyfriend. Turkish Delight—the exotic name appealed but she didn't like the firm red jelly or the perfumey smell. Kit Kat were lovely crisp sticks and Anna liked how they broke apart with a nice clean snap. The jaw-breakers and spongy yellow bananas called to her and the shoestring licorice coiled seductively in long narrow boxes. Anna's mouth spurted saliva as she passed the Lik-a-Maid packets and she sniffed longingly at the Double Bubble box, itching for the promise of the miniature comic that each cube held. The sugar-pink smell of bubble gum stayed with her until she reached the cigarette counter where it was overwhelmed by the wicked and enticing odour of tobacco.

Next to the cigarettes was the till. She always loved the *ting-ting-rring* as she pulled the handle and the satisfying *ching* as the neatly partitioned drawer popped out. She didn't dare pull the handle today, though, and moved quickly around the end of the cash counter into the front of the store.

"Minding the front" was what Anna's family called

working in that part of the store. Since Anna was eight years old she had served coffee and sold cigarettes; by the time she was ten she was "working the back"—the kitchen—as well. She didn't mind making hamburgers and chips. Even though machine-like things didn't usually appeal to Anna, the first time she saw the french fry machine work, she thought, Wow, this is really neat! The french fry machine was a red metal contraption bolted to the kitchen counter. It had a big heavy handle for pressing the potatoes through. She would hang on the handle with all her weight and delight to see the tidy white rectangles emerge. Peeling the potatoes wasn't fun, though, and neither was washing so many dishes.

Washing dishes was often used as punishment. Anna would have to stand for what seemed like forever, shifting from tired foot to tired foot, hands immersed in greasy dishwater. The long counter stretched out beside her with stacks and stacks of thick white plates, cups and saucers. "Dish duty," it was called and it would last as long as it would take for her dad to remember that she was still there. If she dared to ask, "Can I stop now, Dad?" as he rushed past on his way to answer the *ding-ding* of the gas bell outside, he would usually say, "So you think you're working too hard, eh? You don't know what hard work is!" And then he would dole out another hour as if it were just another Hail Mary. She hated dish duty, but she did prefer it to being hit and usually suffered in trapped silence.

Crossing the red and white tile floor in the front of the store, Anna passed the jukebox and paused to look at the titles typed in rows. "North to Alaska," "Yellow Polka Dot Bikini," "Blue Navy" (this was her favourite because of the "...walky-talky-wind-up doll from Toky-oh" which she wished for with all her heart) and "I Will Follow Him," her older sisters' favourite. They would sing it incessantly: "I love him, I love him, I love him...and where he goes I'll follow, I'll follow, I'll follow...he'll always be my true love, my true love, my true love..." until their mother would clamp her hands over her ears and shout, "Enough!" They would begin again with even more fervour and Anna would join in shrilly, enjoying the harassed look on her mother's face. Power. They took it where they could get it.

Anna left the jukebox and sat down in a booth near the front door to wait. She kept looking at herself to make sure she was ready, to make sure she had every-thing, as though a piece of her could suddenly be missing.

One by one, her sisters came out in their haphazard Sunday attire. They snipped and snapped at each other and growled in undertones like grumpy puppies. Eve-ryone was in a foul mood. It was always like that on Sunday mornings. Anna's mom made shushing noises and jiggled her hip to quiet the baby, who was crying irritably.

Anna's father stormed in.

"OK, let's go! Are you all ready? Well, I don't believe it, bunch of lazy bums, why can't you ever be ready on time? Never learn, will you?" Anna couldn't understand why he was carrying on like that. Everyone was here. Everyone was ready.

"Come on, get in the car. Hurry up, we're late! What's the matter with you? Come on, let's go—let's go!"

"Calm down, Leo," Anna's mother admonished anxiously. Just as Anna was climbing into the car, her mother turned and whispered: "Anna, where's your hat?"

Anna could feel her face turn pale and the wild flapping start up again, taking her breath away.

"I forgot...," she said in a thin voice.

Her father's enraged face turned to her and he shouted: "Well, for Christ's sake, don't just stand there, go find something, and hurry up or you'll really get it!" His voice was full of hitting now and Anna ran into the house to look for a scarf. She ploughed through the drawers, throwing things out of her way, wiping away her tears, but everything was a blur.

Her mother came in and saw that there was no hope of finding another kerchief in time. She took Anna by the arm and pulled her into the café. She handed Anna a paper doily and a bobby pin and said, "Here, this will have to do. Hurry now, Dad's at the end of his rope!"

Anna slid into the car. She didn't dare look up. She stared at the white paper circle with the scalloped edges and thought she would die of shame. Everyone at church will know that this is one of those things you put under milkshakes and pies and stuff, she thought in dismay. Everyone will think I am too poor to own a hat. She knew she had to wear a hat in church and she knew there was no getting out of going so she pinned the doily to the top of her head and steeled herself for the humiliation. She cried as quietly as she could. She knew what her father would say if he heard her. "You think you have something to cry about? Here, I'll give you something to cry about." And then he would.

In the seat next to her, seven-year-old Toni scrunched up her face and covered her mouth with one hand to hide her snicker. She pointed at Anna and hunched her shoulders, shaking them up and down in an exaggerated gesture of mirth. Quick as a snake, Anna grabbed Toni's extended finger and hissed, "Shut up!" Toni's imp-face dissolved. She pulled away. She was afraid of Anna. Anna was three years older and strong.

In church Anna managed to forget about the paper doily. She sang the Latin songs and kneeled and stood at all the right times. Her bony knees ached and got purply and bruisy-feeling from the hard wooden benches but she didn't mind much. It was different from having to kneel at home when she was being punished by her father, those long humiliating times in the corner. When the other kids walked by with their friends, she would pretend she was looking for something on the floor.

Going to Communion was always interesting. Anna knew she was supposed to have holy thoughts but she usually found herself trying to sneak a look at other people's tongues. Some of the tongues hung out quivering for a long time and some just shyly darted out and in again with their prize. Anna preferred not to leave hers out too long. Her tongue felt cold and vulnerable and wanted to be tucked back in behind her teeth where it curled up, happily savouring the elusive flavour of the body of Christ. She often felt guilty about wanting another wafer and wishing that they at least be a bit bigger. She knew she was missing the point.

After church something was wrong. She could feel it in the car on the way home. Everyone was too quiet.

When they pulled up in front of the store, the car doors sprang open and everyone started piling out. She felt that she had to get away from the car as fast as possible—as though a bomb was planted in it and the bomb was going to explode any minute.

"Hold it!"

Her dad's voice.

"Don't you move."

The words sliced through Anna and she froze. Only she and Theresa were left sitting in the back seat. In the front seat, the baby on her mother's lap began to wail. Anna looked up and saw her father's finger pointing like the end of a gun into her big sister's face. She felt relief wash over her. Immediately guilt prickled in her gut.

Her dad came around the car and grabbed Theresa by the hair. Then he dragged her over to the garage and started banging her head against the wall. His hands were clutching Theresa's hair on either side of her head and he was screaming in her face.

"What do you think, I'm stupid? You think you can pull one over on me? I'll teach you a thing or two!" Anna's mother looked frantically at Anna and whispered, "What did she do? Oh God, what did she do?"

Anna didn't look at her mother but continued to stare out the window and said flatly: "Nothing."

Her mother got out of the car then and started pleading: "Leo, stop...Oh God, stop...She didn't do anything...Stop it, what did she do...Leo, please..."

Suddenly he stopped and stormed off. It was always like that. Suddenly he'd start and suddenly he'd stop. He was finished—spent. An ejaculation of rage.

Mortal Sins

For my mother

ANNA'S FATHER HAD BEEN in the Roman Catholic priesthood before he quit to marry her mother, so he had his ideas about sex and sin.

One day when Anna was seven years old and her sister Lou was nine, they were playing in the new shower stall. The water wasn't hooked up yet and with the curtain pulled closed, the cubicle made a private little house. They were sitting side by side with their panties around their ankles and a doll blanket over their legs. They were *playing dirty.* That's what Anna and her sisters called it whenever they did anything sexual.

When they heard their father calling, they froze, but not before Anna managed to wiggle her panties up. Then there he was, whipping the shower curtain open and pulling the blanket off their legs. Exposed. Caught. Anna felt shame creep over her face like a hot rash and the words—*little pigs, dirty, sin, mortal sin, going to hell*—burned her ears. There was something else too, something about her dad's intensity and the way he kept smacking and smacking Lou's bare bottom until it was beet red. Anna wasn't caught with her panties down and that seemed to make the difference—she didn't get a licking that time. The word *licking* gave Anna the creeps. It made her think of her dad's tongue hanging out—like a hungry dog. When that picture came into her mind, she had a feeling of bugs crawling all over her skin and she shuddered the way her horse did when flies gathered on his flanks.

What Anna's father said about going to hell scared her. Questions began to form in her mind. What did he mean by that? I know that if you die with a mortal sin on your soul you go straight to hell, but I thought kids couldn't do mortal sins. The mortal sins in the Ten Commandments are about killing and there is something about your neighbour's wife. Anna could not imagine ever killing anyone and she didn't know what the other commandment meant. I'd better ask my mom about mortal sins just to be sure, she thought.

Her mother was ironing.

"Mom, is playing dirty a venial sin or a mortal sin and will I go to hell if I die with it on my soul?"

Anna's mother paused and looked intently at Anna before she continued ironing, then replied in a calm voice, "Yes, Anna, it's a mortal sin but you don't have to stop doing it...just be sure to confess it."

Anna didn't understand the look on her mother's face—a kind of half-smile on her lips and a sparkle in her eyes. It was a look that Anna had never seen before. Really devilish, Anna thought.

It was clear to Anna in that moment that her mother had some kind of power over God to be able to bend the rules like that. What her mother had said didn't make sense to Anna, but at the same time, seemed right somehow.

"But what do I call it?" Anna asked. Surely she couldn't say *playing dirty* to the priest!

"You call it a sin of immodesty," her mother replied, without altering the rhythm of the iron. Anna watched for a moment, wondering how her mother managed to keep her fingers out of the way so perfectly each time. Her fingers flew lightly over the skirt she was working on, smoothing out corners and holding down pleats with the steel point of the iron in hot pursuit.

"Sin of immodesty, sin of immodesty, sin of immodesty..." Anna repeated this impressive grown-up phrase three times on the out-breath and three more times on the in-breath, until she knew she wouldn't forget it. The words pleased her, and with the chanting, she felt the shame melt away. She felt a stillness inside like a storm had passed and the sun was breaking through the clouds. From this quiet place she felt she could see everything clearly. She would add them up carefully, her sins of immodesty, then just to be sure that she was never caught with one on her soul (it was always possible to be hit by a car on the way to church), she would add ten to the total. So, she thought, three this week, plus ten—that's thirteen. She felt very clever.

"Bless me, Father, for I have sinned and it has been one week since my last confession and these are my sins...I took a chocolate bar from the store without asking, I lied to my Mom about it, I committed thirteen sins of immodesty, I said a swear word and that's all, Father."

Anna usually tried to slip the sins of immodesty casually into the middle of her confession so that they wouldn't stand out among the rest. The priest didn't seem to notice. He just gave her the usual few Hail Marys and the occasional Our Father, so after a few weeks Anna wasn't even nervous any more. She continued to confess in this way until she was twelve—until the time the new priest came to her church, that awful time when Father Leroux was sick. Anna was used to Father Leroux and didn't like the idea of a stranger-priest at all. Very reluctantly, when her turn came, she stepped into the little closet and knelt. She recited her confession in her usual way and everything seemed normal until she reached the part about the sins of immodesty.

"What was that, dear?"

Anna froze.

"Did you say *twelve* sins of immodesty, dear?"

"Yes, Father."

"Were you by yourself when you committed these sins?"

"Yes, Father."

"What were you wearing, dear? Did you have your clothes off?"

"Well, sort of...uh, some of them..." Anna felt she had to answer the priest's questions. She felt trapped. Her thoughts flew around in her mind like frightened birds trying to escape. Oh God, she thought, I can't explain to him that ten of them never happened and I can't just make up stuff. She felt all hot and sweaty and she could hardly breathe.

"Now tell me exactly what you did, dear...What was that?...Say that again, dear...I can't quite hear you."

Anna wanted to die. He made her repeat her answers over and over until finally she started to cry.

"You can go now," he said in a tight and breathy voice. It seemed to Anna as though his face was pressed too close and the fine mesh screen separating them was vibrating in a strange rhythmic way. He didn't even give her any penance.

Anna burst out of the dark closet and ran out of the church. She was supposed to go back to her catechism class, but she felt exposed, as though the other kids would be able to see her sins hanging out of her in some obscene way. She felt covered in hot sticky shame and she ran and ran until she was almost home. By the time she had slowed down to a walk the thoughts and feelings swirling around inside her had turned into a grey mist which got thinner and thinner until it fragmented and finally trailed in diaphanous wisps into a dark corner of herself.

Kitty Love

For Jeffrey

THERE WAS VERY LITTLE MODESTY in Anna's family. She had five sisters. So many sisters, so many naked bodies—baby chub to nubile nymph. There were no brothers to make them feel blank like baby dolls and Barbie dolls, to point out what they didn't have. Anna knew that she and her sisters had things alright. They had bums and cracks and pussies and titties and nipples and pennies and pee holes and bum holes and chiz. Chiz was the stuff that dried on the crotch of her panties—if it got on her hands she could still smell it hours later when she put her fingers right to her nose and breathed in. Anna would often do this, finding her own smell deeply reassuring.

The girls played and fought and lounged around in varying states of undress, reading comic books and Nancy Drew mysteries. In this harem-like atmosphere they compared breast size the way other families measured growth spurts on the wall. Anna felt the hard swollen circle underneath the soft nipple of first her older sisters', and then her own, brand-new breasts. "Feel my penny!" she announced proudly when her titties finally formed that round hardness inside, that tender promise of voluptuousness.

Anna had her first orgasm when she was nine years old. She was marking the goods, the boxes of canned food that always arrived on Saturdays. Her job was to mark the prices on the tops of the tins with a black grease pencil, then stack them neatly on the shelves.

On this particular Saturday, she was squatting behind the boxes and a bored little fingernail was skimming back and forth, back and forth, over the crotch of her nylon panties. At first she was daydreaming; then she felt more interested in what her finger was doing. It was like scratching a really good itch which just got itchier and itchier, but this feeling was more pleasant, had more promise to it. Then there was an almost-too-much-but-definitely-don't-stop feeling followed by a blip-blip-bubbling over and spilling out...

After that time, Anna would lie in bed at night, just before she slept, and arrange her body in the princess position—on her back, arms bent at the elbow and delicately placed up over her head, with the palms of her hands turned up. She would turn her face slightly to the side, toward the middle of the room and the window. The position of her legs was the most important. She would place them just so, with one leg straight, and the other leg bent with toes pointed perfectly at the knee. Just like a ballerina, Anna thought.

Thus she would lie, a princess awaiting her prince—for surely this was how a princess would sleep all the night through. Anna was always disappointed in herself when she woke in the morning, inevitably curled up in an undignified ball.

This ritual was performed in the event that a prince might come through the window—she never knew when he would arrive and she had to be ready—to kiss her awake. Not on the mouth, though...it was always on those other lips, the secret hungry ones, that she imagined being kissed.

Anna learned about this kind of kissing from her favourite cat, Tiger. Sometimes Tiger would crawl beneath the covers and between Anna's legs. Settled there, he would knead gently with his soft paws and root for the little nipple hidden in the sweet earth-smell there, rough tongue searching, finding, sucking...

Dreaming of her prince, Anna would come and then pull herself away immediately, the electric shoots of pleasure too intense. Soon, however, the sensations would fade and there he'd be again, purring rhythmically, the steadiest lover. And again, and again…

Anna always tired of this activity first, then she would reject her cat coldly, send him out of her bed, and sleep like an angel, cheeks pink with after-love.

The Change

For my dad

ANNA'S DAD ALWAYS SAID that children, like horses, need a place to run free. In the summer, other families hung around the subdivision and went out to the lake on weekends, but day trips to the public beach were not for Anna's family. As soon as school was out, her dad said, "What we all need is a change!" Then he hired someone to mind the store that they owned, and he packed up the station wagon. He stacked the mattresses from their beds on top of the car while Anna's mom packed boxes and boxes of clothes and food. Anna's dad was always ready first and sat in the car, honking the horn and shouting out the window, "C'mon, let's go, let's *go*!" Finally, Anna and her five sisters and her mom all piled in and they'd set out on their big adventure.

In Anna's mind, the drive usually took about forever because Anna's dad was never satisfied unless they found a place that was as far away as possible. It had to be completely wild. It had to be the perfect spot. They drove north, up the island, as far as the pavement lasted and then he chose old logging roads that were hardly roads at all. Sometimes after driving up an overgrown dirt track which was no more than two ruts with long grass on the middle hump scraping the bottom of the car, they reached a dead end and had to back out for what seemed like hours. After a few of these dead ends, Anna began feeling anxious. Any minute now, Mom's going to start complaining like crazy, she thought. That was the part Anna didn't like because her mom and dad fought so much—Anna's mother asking every half hour, "Where exactly are we, Leo?" Even after so many dead ends her dad insisted that he knew exactly where they were. He didn't give in and never admitted to being one little bit lost. Anna usually believed him. He had a way of saying it that was so convincing. Anna's mother always gave up in the end and, after a lot of eye-rolling, sat with her arms crossed and glared out the side window.

During these long trips Anna and her sisters played "I Spy" and "On My Way to Africa" or they sang "My Name Is Jon Jonson" or "I Went To The Animal Fair."

These were both songs that they could repeat over and over and that, they knew, drove their mother crazy. Especially the end of the Animal Fair one. They sang the last line: "...the monk, the monk, the monk, the monk..." until she begged them to stop. It was especially funny because she had been the one to teach them those songs.

When the games and songs wore out, there they were, six kids panting like puppies in the heat, dust from the open windows making their hair turn white and their teeth gritty. Sometimes they snarled and snapped at each other, irritable from the hours of sitting in the hot car. Anna's father, busy concentrating on missing the enormous pot-holes, seemed not to notice. At home, none of this quibbling would have been tolerated, but once they were on the road, on their big adventure, something about him changed. He just wasn't scary any more. The way he usually was.

Sometimes they came across old wooden trestle bridges that spanned deep chasms. Each time, Anna's mother insisted on being let out of the car to cross on foot. Anna's dad refused to stop the car until her mother became almost hysterical. Her hands flapping around in the air like frightened birds, her eyes wide, she begged him to stop and when he finally did, she got out of the car.

"Damn you!" She cursed him under her breath as she slammed the door. Then Anna's mother watched the car, with all of them in it, cross the bridge. Once they were safely across she picked her way, in obvious terror, over the big beams. Anna often wondered why, if her mother was so certain that the bridge wouldn't hold the weight of the car, she left all her kids in it. Anna turned around and watched out the back window. Seeing her mother standing there in the middle of the road, looking very small and disappearing in a cloud of dust, was somehow a familiar feeling. It seemed her mother always disappeared when things got scary. Anna also felt afraid crossing those bridges, but she never dared admit it. Her father would make a disgusted snorting noise under his breath and call her mother a coward. Anna didn't want to be anything like her mother. She wanted to be just like her dad.

By the time the perfect spot was finally found, Anna and her sisters were hanging out the windows whimpering in anticipation and bouncing on the seats with their need to pee. To listen to her dad's exclamations, anyone would think they'd arrived at a palace. "Oh my God, will you look at this!" he'd exclaim. "Isn't this beautiful! Look at that water! Will you look at that beach! This is it. The perfect spot!" He leaped out of the car, already in his bathing trunks, prepared for this moment, and ran splashing into the lake. He dove right in and came up an unbelievable distance away and swam out and out and out. From the beach they could hear his shouts. "Come on! The water's so warm!" No matter how weedy or muddy or cold it really was, his enthusiasm eventually drew them all in.

Then it was time to set up camp and he put Anna, and all the kids that were old enough to walk, to work collecting firewood and pitching tents. It never felt like work to Anna. Her dad made it all seem like fun. Every little stick of wood dumped on the pile was praised. Every blow to a tent peg was exclaimed about. By the time camp was made, a tent area cleared and shelves built into the trees with clothes-lines strung between, Anna felt like Tarzana, the Jungle Girl. Slivers and aching muscles were prizes to boast about.

"Let's feel those muscles!" her dad said and Anna clenched her fists and showed her muscles with all her might.

This camp was to be their new home for the summer, rain or shine. From the moment they arrived, Anna and her sisters became water babies. Naked as the sky, day in, day out. Half a dozen sun-browned, sugar cookie bums with dried sand stuck on round cheeks in two perfect circles. Between bouts of wild play or long quiet hours collecting bright pebbles (which always lost their jewel shine when they dried), Anna collapsed on the hot sand and slid into and out of dreamy sleeps. Then the sound of the others splashing seductively or shrieking in the ecstasy of some game lured her back and, like a lizard, she belly-crawled down to the water's lapping edge and slipped back into the lake. A warm blue womb.

All of their sounds were acceptable here. Ear-piercing screaming, hoot-hoot-hooting, sudden shrieks and wails were absorbed utterly by the trees and water and sky. They were never shushed and Anna's dad would never transform, as he did at home, into the monster.

Periodically, during the days, the need for food called them out of the water and they rummaged through the boxes for whatever they could find. They gobbled like starving animals, tearing chunks of bread from the loaves with their hands, sand in everything. Crunch, crunch. Then, the painfully long half-hour wait until they could go back in to swim. They played in the shallows, asking plaintively every few minutes, "Is it time yet?"

Finally, at sunset, shivering and prune-fingered, Anna and her sisters sat around the fire, roasted hot dogs and marshmallows on long thin poles that they cut themselves, and told each other ghost stories. Their favourite was "...and now he's coming up the stairs...'I want my liver back!'...and now he's on the top step...'I want my liver back!'...and now he's outside your bedroom door..."

When at last they tumbled sleepily into their tent, Anna never remembered falling asleep, just seeing the sun coming warm through the canvas in the morning and feeling the strong need to pee. Sometimes, in the night, Anna woke up and struggled with her full bladder before finally giving in and going outside to pee. It was very scary outside. There were little yellow eyes out there watching her intently. It was hard not to pee on her feet because she dared not look down and anyway, it was too dark to see in which direction the stream was flowing. Peeing into sand was best. Hardly any splash. There was never any outhouse, not even for *number two*. And no toilet paper. "Just use leaves," Anna's father instructed, and so they did.

One night, after they had all slipped to dream, Anna's dad came into the tent and whispered, "Who wants to go for a midnight swim?" There was something in his voice, that special voice he used, that reached out to Anna. It was so full of adventure, so full of promises! Even though sleep pulled at her seductively, she couldn't resist that voice. It called to her, told her that she was special, that she was brave.

She dragged her sleepy body out of the warm blankets, stumbled over the grumbling bodies of her sisters and walked out shivering into the night. Everything was so quiet. The lake lay still and black under the big moon and her father stood there, a dark silhouette at the water's edge. "That's my girl, come on, let's go!" he said. Still half asleep, Anna pulled off her clothes and ran splashing into the lake with her dad. They swam out, following the moon path on the water. He didn't swim too far ahead, as he sometimes did in the day, but swam the breast stroke alongside her, the only sounds their bodies moving through the liquid dark and their breath blowing out like small whales. After the cool night air, the water was warm satin against her skin. Anna would never have dared go out so far in the day as they did that night. She couldn't see the shore, only the moonlight on the inky surface ahead of her and her father next to her. She felt safe and strong, like she could swim forever. When they circled back and pulled their bodies out onto the beach, her dad wrapped her immediately in a big towel. Then he rubbed her head and arms and legs hard until her skin tingled and her shivering stopped.

"Good for you," he said. "Now didn't that feel great? Now we're going to have a good sleep!" Climbing back into her pants and layers of shirts and sweaters, Anna didn't mind how the cloth and sand stuck to her chilly damp skin. She felt warm on the inside. In the morning, the moonlight swim felt like a dream until her dad said, "Boy, did you guys miss a good swim last night!" and he threw her a wink.

At the end of summer, they began to clear out the campsite and Anna felt such sadness. In the car on the long drive home, everyone was strangely quiet. Anna dreaded returning to their lives in the store. Anxiety, that prickly little creature that had been quiet all summer, began to stir fretfully in her chest once more. Her father, she knew, would change when they got back.

Nanny Goat
and Billy Goat

For Nanny

WHEN ANNA WAS A LITTLE GIRL, her family called her Nanny Goat. This was her everyday name from the time she was an infant until she was thirteen years old. Anna got this nickname from her sister, Louise, who was only two years old when Anna was born. Louise couldn't pronounce "Anna"; all she could say was "Na Na." Na Na evolved into Nanny, which eventually became Nanny Goat. Anna became so used to this nickname that it never occurred to her that it was odd. On her thirteenth birthday, however, her father, who was always very conscious of public opinion, insisted that the family start calling Anna by her given name.

This felt strange to Anna at first—it was as though she wasn't quite sure who *Anna* was, but eventually she became used to her true name. Over the years, when in a teasing or affectionate mood, one of her family members, even her father from time to time, would call her Nanny Goat. She felt warm inside when this happened, like her young self was remembered.

Nanny's father had six daughters and no sons. She was his boy. A tomboy. Such an interesting term—she wondered if it came from tom cat. Toms strutted around, got into fights and were very interested in sex. That was Nanny.

Nanny would do almost anything not to be like her mother or two older sisters. They were always *getting it* from her dad. Nanny would do things—hard things, like play with garter snakes—just to toughen herself up. She refused to cry or show that she was afraid—ever. She soon noticed that if she didn't cry when her dad was hitting her, he stopped sooner. Anna would do almost anything to stay in his good books. She learned how to do and say little things to please him. She also learned how to lie. She became very, very good at it. This combination—pleasing him when she could and lying when she could not—spared her a lot of beatings. It also meant that her dad would usually choose her to accompany him whenever there were fun things to do, like working in the garage or making things out of wood. He also taught her how to do push-ups and how to arm wrestle so that she could beat even the boys her age, and he often played rough-and-tumble games with her. Sometimes he was too rough but she never let on. Nanny's dad still came after her at times though, no matter how hard she tried. If she happened to be within reach when he was on the warpath, she *got it*, just like her mother and sisters.

One day after watching "My Favorite Martian" on TV, Nanny began getting a picture in her mind of herself with two antennae sticking out of her head. These feelers were invisible but she could sense them quivering and snaking around whenever danger was near. After a while it was as though they really worked. She could feel a storm brewing a mile away.

Nanny spent her childhood trying to gain her father's approval. Her sisters hated her for this and called her a *suck-hole*. "You've got him wrapped around your little finger," they'd sneer at her. Part of her felt embarrassed when they said this and part of her couldn't believe how dumb they were. I don't understand how they could be stupid enough to try to stand up to him, she thought.

When Nanny was eleven, a new girl came to her school. Not only was the girl new, and therefore desirable, but she was from South Africa, and her accent gave her an exotic quality that made her the most sought-after friend in Nanny's class. The way the new girl shaped her lips around words and the delightful way that the words came out, as though each was a precisely crafted jewel, sent thrills through Nanny. And the new girl had a bouncy walk which made her bobbed hair swing around her face, just like in the Breck Girl shampoo commercials on TV. Nanny was fascinated with the new girl's hair. It was so blonde that it was almost white. Just looking at that hair made Nanny feel like writing a poem. Nanny wanted her. She wanted her so badly that she was willing to do almost anything to get her. But Nanny felt hopeless about it. Why would the new girl pick *me* for a friend? she thought dismally. It seemed to Nanny that the other girls were much more interesting.

The second day after the new girl arrived, Nanny was in the washroom at recess and overheard two girls talking about Wilamena—that was her name. It didn't seem a real name to Nanny, but like something she would read in a book. The girls were saying in excited voices that Wilamena sounded so neat when she talked and did you know that she had her own horse? Nanny took this information and twisted it a little. That day at lunch, she approached Wilamena and told her that some of the other girls were talking about her, that they had said they didn't like her, but would pretend to be her friend so that they could ride her horse. Nanny then announced that she, too, had a horse (it was actually her sister's horse, but she left that part out), and that she knew how fickle friends could be. Nanny felt guilty because saying this really worked. Wilamena's dear face went all dark and she frowned and said, "I really hate girls like that."

"Me too," Nanny said. Then Wilamena asked if Nanny would like to come over to her house after school that day. Nanny was in heaven. I'll probably go to hell for such a rotten lie, she thought, but I don't care.

On this day, Nanny needed the perfect outfit and knew it was not likely to be found. She did not have much to choose from—her family was poor and she often had only hand-me-downs. Nanny's parents never mentioned that they were poor, however, and they always let their children know that they were not like the other families in the neighbourhood. They held this high opinion of themselves because her father did not work at the mill like all the other dads. He and Nanny's mother ran a café, gas station and general store on the highway on the outskirts of the small town. They were self-employed and this, in her parents' eyes, gave them class. The other factor that Nanny's parents felt gave them class was that they were from the east, from the big city of Montreal, and had only moved to the small west coast town in recent years. Although they were never short of food—they did live in the back of a café, after all—it seemed to Nanny that the other kids in the neighbourhood always had nice things, especially the latest Barbies with all the tiny perfect accessories. That's what Nanny loved about Barbie—her clothes.

By the time Nanny got home after school she was beside herself with excitement. A new friend! She tore off her blue corduroy jumper, almost ripped off the buttons on the back of her white blouse, and rummaged through the pile of laundry. Clothes flew as she searched desperately for something to wear. It had to be just right. Nanny had always been like that about clothes—each event was a performance and required the exact right costume. Sometimes things fell into place fairly quickly, and sometimes she would get into a changing frenzy and every article of clothing she owned ended up in heaps all over the room and nothing was perfect enough for the occasion.

This particular day was a disaster. There were hardly any clean clothes and she could not find one pair of slacks. Nanny was desperate to change and get out the door before someone found a chore for her to do in the café. She was at the point where she would wear almost anything. In a panic she went to her mother for help. Nanny's mother was always slightly distracted, as though, with six kids to raise and a store to run, she was perpetually in-between one moment and the next and never really *there*. Getting her attention was an art. It was also risky because, all too often, coming into her field of awareness meant being assigned a chore. Nanny gathered all her energy, all the intensity of her desire and her need, and stormed into her mother's space—that vague other world that she occupied—and delivered her plea for something to wear. Nanny's mother focused on her for a brief moment, then gestured toward the shelves where the school supplies and fishing tackle were displayed.

"There's a pair of jeans there," she said. "You can have them if they fit."

The jeans fit all right, but they were boys' jeans. With a zipper down the front. This was definitely not OK. Girls' pants had a side-zipper and boys' pants had a fly. That was that. It was unthinkable that she should wear boys' jeans. The very idea made her think of dinks and the way boys peed. Nanny knew what a fly was for. She didn't have to have brothers to know that. She decided to wear them, her desire to be with Wilamena overcoming her fear of humiliation. She chose an old shirt of her dad's to go over top—the shirt tails came almost to her knees—and ran out the door. Wilamena's house was about half a mile away, not far on horseback. Nanny headed out to the barn, which was really just a shed built onto the house behind the café, to get her sister's horse. Louise isn't home to ask and doesn't seem to care whether I ride the horse or not, Nanny thought. She's more interested in boys than horses, and anyway, Dad's usually on my side about the horse.

"Good for you for exercising him! Your sister's so damn lazy!" her dad would say. It was Louise who had to feed the horse and brush him down and get up in the middle of the night to find him when he got out of the yard—even if it was Nanny who had left the gate unlatched. She *had* left the gate unlatched just the other day and Louise had been smacked across the head for it. "Maybe *that* will help you remember!" her dad had said. Guilt ran like little spiders over Nanny's skin, but she brushed the feeling away. What's the point of owning up? Nanny thought. Louise already got smacked and I'll get smacked for sure if I admit to it. Nanny reminded herself about the time Louise had come home with a big red mark on her neck and begged Nanny to tell their dad that Sammy had nipped her. Sammy (that was the horse's nickname—his real name was Samourzem which Nanny's dad said meant *love* in Arabic) was three-quarters Arabian and one-quarter thoroughbred. He had lots of spirit but had never kicked or bit anyone.

When Louise showed Nanny the blotch and told her that she had gotten it from her boyfriend, Nanny was disgusted.

"Ew, gross!" Nanny screwed up her face. "What *is* that?"

"It's a hickey, dummy," Louise said, rolling her eyes.

Right, like I'm really stupid for not knowing, Nanny thought. She did feel stupid, but didn't show it. Then Louise bared her neck so Nanny could get a closer look. Louise seemed proud of the hickey. It made Nanny think of leeches. "OK, I'll back you up on the horse story," she said. "But you owe me one."

As soon as Nanny unlatched the gate, the horse tossed his head and blew air through his big soft lips to make a lovely vibrating sound in greeting. He danced over to Nanny and pushed at her with his nose, almost knocking her off her feet. "OK, OK," she murmered as she adjusted the bridle over his head, slipped her thumb in behind his back teeth, and slid the bit into place.

With a running leap, Nanny was on Sammy's broad back and in moments, she was out the side gate and thundering down the highway with the wind in her face. She reminded herself to keep her lips closed tightly together to stop the bugs from flying in and kept a firm grip on the reins. Sammy particularly enjoyed running along the highway. Far from being spooked by the cars whizzing by, he would speed up each time a car approached and race with it.

It took all Nanny's strength to turn him off the highway. Slowing him down to a rolling canter, she headed into the subdivision toward Wilamena's house. When Nanny came up the driveway, she slid off onto the ground and looked up to see her new friend standing, in all her glory, on the front steps. Immediately Nanny noticed that Wilamena was wearing boys' jeans. The very first thing Wilemena said was, "Hey, are those boys' jeans?"

"Of course," Nanny said nonchalantly.

"I would never wear girls' jeans—they are so dumb."

"Yeah, sissy pants," Nanny replied. They were fast friends from that moment on and Nanny never wore a side-zipper again in Wilamena's presence.

Wilamena also had a family nickname. Her family called her Billy. Nanny's family called her Billy Goat.

Nanny and Billy rode their horses up and down the subdivision streets a world apart from all the other kids. From horseback they could look down their noses at people. They always rode bare-back. Nanny loved the feeling of Sammy's powerful muscles moving between her legs. The horse was big and dusty-warm and rolled beneath her like an ocean. She could feel the tension gathering there, the horse's desire to explode into motion. She loved to see the long cords of muscle swelling on his shiny black neck as she pulled back on the reins, holding him in check, until her own desire for the rush of speed peaked and with a firm squeeze of her thighs she would release him. The fear and the pleasure, the rhythmic drumming of his hooves on the ground and the wind in her ears, thrilled through her like a song. The sheer power was intoxicating and after a long ride she would dismount, her face hot, her breath coming hard. She would be giddy and weak in the knees—a good feeling.

When Nanny and Billy weren't on horseback, they explored the trails in the bush behind the café. They imagined them to be cougar trails and frightened each other with "sightings" of long tawny shapes slinking through the trees. Cougars *were* sometimes sighted in the area and whenever they were, Old Man Black, the cougar hunter, would arrive at the café with his slack-lipped, long-eared hounds drooling and whining in their cages on the back of his flat-bed truck. He would always order a Leo the Lion burger. This was Nanny's dad's special creation and it had two hamburger patties and two slices of bacon, topped with a fried weiner split down the middle. Washing the burger down with cup after cup of coffee, Old Man Black would tell cougar tales while Nanny and Billy sat on the adjoining stools, elbows propped on the counter and chins resting in their hands, drinking in every word.

One summer, Old Man Black and his hounds hunted a cougar down on Hudson's farm just a quarter mile up the road from the café. Billy was staying over at Nanny's that night and they could hear the hounds baying as they lay trying to sleep. The eerie howling both frightened and excited them and they began making mournful wailing sounds of their own under the covers until Nanny's dad thumped his fist on the door and shouted, "Hey, get to sleep in there!" in his *watch out* voice. Nanny ran with the cougar in her dreams that night.

Hudson's farm was a favourite hang-out for Nanny and Billy. They would leap off fences onto the backs of the doe-eyed milking cows but were never able to stay on long. It wasn't anything like being on horseback; the skin on the cows' backs slid precariously from side to side and the protruding ridge of the bovine spines hurt in that tender spot between the girls' legs.

Mr. and Mrs. Hudson were old. Nanny thought their faces looked like dried-up apples. They were kind faces, though, and they were usually framed by some funny old hat. The Hudsons' own kids were all grown and they always welcomed Nanny and Billy. Nanny especially loved bottle-feeding the orphaned lambs in the spring, and as long as the girls were careful, they were allowed to pick up the chicks that ran helter-skelter around the hen yard like tiny yellow tumble-weeds in a wind.

The one thing that the girls were not supposed to do was tease the two cranky old Clydesdales. Sometimes though, they couldn't resist. Nanny and Billy would yelp and dance wildly about and throw pine cones which bounced like insects off the Clydesdales' broad behinds. The horses would usually ignore them. One day, Nanny watched them pulling at the grass with their big yellow teeth and shifting from one shaggy foot to the other. They look bored as can be, she thought, and she became even more determined to get a reaction. She ran up close, waved her arms around and screeched. Suddenly, the horse closest to her wheeled around and with ears laid flat, thundered after her.

"RUN!" Billy screamed.

Nanny didn't check over her shoulder as she ran. She could hear the drumming of the big hooves and the horse's breath was loud in her ears by the time she reached the fence. Leaping up, she placed both hands on the top rail and vaulted over sideways. When she hit the ground on the other side, Billy was already there.

"You almost didn't make it in time!" her friend panted with her eyes wide.

They held their hands over their thumping hearts as they watched the big mare stomp and snort and then turn away. Nanny shivered as she realized how close they had come to having their heads crushed—like grapes, she thought—under those great hooves.

That was the last time they teased the Clydesdales, but Nanny and Billy had many other ways of expending their excess energy. They would wrestle each other to the ground in rough-and-tumble games. Or they played "I dare you" and there was nothing they wouldn't dare to do. Once, Billy dared Nanny to kiss a fat green slug. Nanny did, even though she thought the slug was gross and wet-looking. She didn't realize that the slime would stick to her lips. She rubbed at them all day but it wouldn't rub off.

Nanny and Billy guarded each other jealously from any attempts made by other kids to join them on their adventures. To get rid of a classmate who wanted to play with them, they would suggest a horse manure fight. Suddenly the girl would remember some errand she had to do and leave. It worked every time.

They carried a few balls of dried horse manure in

their pockets as ready ammunition. Hiding behind the big rock in the field across from the café, they would ambush the boys on their way home from school. If a boy walked by on his own, Nanny and Billy would leap out screaming like banshees, run him down and cram the balls of dried horse manure into his mouth. Later, when they encountered their victim at school, they would say under their breath, "Eat shit," and the boy would scuttle away from them in terror.

There was one boy in particular that Nanny and Billy liked to pick on. His name was Dicky Dehagen. Dicky was a fat boy with red hair and freckles and he was fun to pick on because he always cried. They tripped him when he stepped off the bus, put tacks on his seat at school and stomped on his kites before he could get them off the ground.

They also practised saying the word *fuck* in every possible tone and inflection. They added *fuck* to their sentences as often as possible. "No-fucking-way," they would say, or "Nice-fucking-day." Nanny and Billy took great pleasure in their own and each other's wickedness.

Nanny secretly hoped that she would never start her period. Nanny's older sisters had started at eleven. She saw what happened to them and she did not want it to happen to her. "My sisters have turned boy-crazy," Nanny told Billy. Being boy-crazy was a form of insanity that caused her sisters to sit in front of the mirror for hours. When they weren't backcombing their hair, they were putting it up in buns or wrapping it in wire rollers. Sometimes they would tie a scarf over the rollers, put on make-up and go downtown. I wouldn't be caught dead, Nanny thought. Now and then Nanny would chase her sisters around the yard with garter snakes. Her sisters would squeal and run and tell her that she was disgusting and *why didn't she just grow up*! Nanny never wanted to grow up.

Customers in the café often told Nanny that she was pretty and this always annoyed her. *Girls* were pretty and Nanny didn't like to think of herself as a girl. She tried hard to ignore the small buds poking out of her T-shirts.

"I hate boys to death!" Nanny confided fiercely to Billy one day.

"Yeah, boys are pigs," Billy replied and proceeded to make snorting and grunting noises which sent them both into hysterics. From then on, they made a point of making loud piggy noises whenever they saw a boy. With blind determination, Nanny and Billy ignored the different way that some of the older boys had begun looking at them. They had eyes only for each other.

Billy was short and stocky with a quick abrupt way of moving that Nanny loved. Nanny was consumed with a love for Billy that forgave all faults and made Billy perfect. Billy had a kind of power over Nanny. Nanny was adoring—Billy was the adored. At times Billy would be cool with Nanny or scorn her, and at those times Nanny suffered. She poured all her energy into charming and pleasing Billy. Billy was charmed and pleased as it suited her.

By the time Nanny and Billy were thirteen, boys were no less disgusting to them, but had begun to take on a certain fascination. More and more often, their games became focused around activities that would get the boys' attention. Long hours were spent devising plans to *get them*. One day, Billy dared Nanny to kiss one.

"Ew, gross! You are disgusting!" Nanny said and made a dramatic show of pretending to put her finger down her throat while making convincing gagging noises.

"I dare you!" Billy challenged.

"Yeah, well, I dare *you*!" Nanny replied, her feet placed wide and her hands on her hips.

Neither of the girls was willing to be out-done, so after school that day they hid behind the bus stop as the rest of the kids got off the bus. The boys always sat at the back of the bus so by the time they began to unload the girls were well hidden. The first boy to step down was Dicky Dehagen. Nanny and Billy looked at each other and simultaneously did the finger-down-the-throat gesture and let him walk by. The last boy off the bus was Hank Lundstrom. Hank was small for his age with honey-coloured hair that fell in voluptuous curls over his forehead. He had round cheeks and pretty red lips and reminded Nanny of the boy angels in the pictures in her catechism books. The girls looked at each other and nodded.

"I double-dare you," Billy shouted as they chased him down. They had never chased Hank before and he looked confused as he stumbled along with his arms loaded down with books. It didn't take Nanny and Billy long to catch him. They threw him to the ground, and instead of stuffing horse manure down his throat, they both kissed him. They took turns holding him down for each other. Then they let him up and they ran away while he just stood staring after them with wide blue eyes. Hank hadn't struggled much and Nanny didn't feel the way she usually did after catching a boy. This is weird, she thought, when they finally stopped to catch their breath. She felt embarrassed and didn't know why she and Billy had been the ones to run. Nanny and Billy walked back to the bus stop to get their books in silence. They concentrated hard on kicking small stones with the blunt rubber toes of their Converse All-Stars, sending the stones skipping and spinning along the pavement in front of them.

When the holidays came, Nanny and Billy spent every waking hour together, and slept over every chance they got. One steamy summer night, Nanny was sleeping over at Billy's house. Nanny loved Billy's room because it was in the attic and had sloping ceilings which made it feel like their very own little house. There was a tiny window which looked out over the fields and from up so high, all the cows and horses looked like tiny plastic farm toys. Nanny and Billy were both wearing new cotton PJs—boys' pyjamas, blue, with cowboys galloping over them, bought that very day at Woolworth's and still creased from the packaging. They had gone to the barber shop that day, too, and had brandnew haircuts—pixie-cuts with ducktails at the back. Nanny and Billy thought themselves very spiffy.

Fresh from their baths, they lay side by side with their arms folded behind their heads, stared at the attic ceiling, and talked about how hot it was.

It was too hot to sleep. Nanny wanted to take her pyjamas off. Partly because it was hot, partly because she wanted Billy to do the same. Nanny was curious about Billy's breasts. She couldn't tell, looking at Billy in her clothes, whose breasts were bigger. Nanny hoped Billy's were, but she didn't want her own to be *smaller,* either. Nanny wanted them both to be *exactly* the same size. She wanted everything about them to be the same, forever.

Finally, Nanny remarked, "It's way too hot in here," and pulled her pyjama top off over her head. Then she turned quickly and lay on her stomach with her face turned away. She could hear Billy taking her top off too. After a while, Nanny said, "It's too hot for any pyjamas," and she sat up on the edge of the bed and slid her bottoms off. She flopped back down on her tummy.

"Yeah," Billy said and threw *her* bottoms onto the floor.

For a long moment, Nanny just lay there. Then her curiosity peaked and in the most casual movement she could manage, she rolled over onto her side, facing her friend. To Nanny's surprise, Billy was already lying facing her, but her eyes were closed as though she were asleep. Nanny badly wanted to look at her friend's body but was afraid Billy would open her eyes and catch her looking. Nanny closed her eyes too.

Their faces were inches apart, sharing a pillow, and Nanny could feel Billy's breath on her lips—she smelled like hamburgers, which is what they had eaten for dinner. Nanny began to feel hungry—sort of. She inched her head a little closer and grumbled, "Stop hogging the pillow, greedy-guts." Billy giggled and pressed her face against Nanny's, smushing their noses together, and said, "There, is that better?" Instead of triggering the usual tug-of-war over the pillow, they froze with their lips and noses touching. At first, Nanny held her breath, and then she noticed Billy's breathing. It was getting louder and came in short little bursts which exploded like warm clouds on Nanny's face. Suddenly Nanny couldn't hold her own breath any longer and when she let it go a small sound emerged with it. A sound Nanny had never heard come from herself before. Like a small hungry creature inside her was crying for something. A heat began to grow deep in

Nanny's belly—again, something she'd never felt before—and it was strong. It was a feeling that demanded
something—like hunger, yes, but much, much stronger.
Nanny felt heat coming from Billy too, and it created
a pull like a magnet between their bodies. Without
knowing that she had moved, without planning to at
all, Nanny found her hips pushing forward into Billy's.
The pull seemed to come and go, their hips pushed and
then receded, pushed and then receded, over and over
in a rhythmic wave.

Nanny had had sexual feelings before. She knew how
to make herself come by running her finger back and
forth over the crotch of her panties, and did so often
when she was by herself. This was different. She had
never felt this particular feeling before, this compelling
movement toward another person's body. She became
utterly lost in the sensation. There was no more Nanny,
no more Billy, just bodies pushing and lips, closed as
tight as eyes, pressing together hard.

Nanny felt perspiration sticky between her thighs.
Her hands felt sweat on Billy's back. They didn't stroke
each other but held on tight. The heat made their
bodies slippery. They began to slide over each other like
two buttery seals. Nanny wanted to do something more
but did not have any idea what. She wanted to be closer
to Billy, to climb inside her. Finally, having exhausted
the possibilities, their breathing slowed, they lay still,
and they fell into a deep sleep.

In the middle of the night, Nanny woke up with her lower belly aching fiercely. She went to the bathroom to pee. When she stood up to flush, she saw that the water in the toilet bowl was bright red.

"Oh, shit, fuck, piss, damn!" Stuffing some toilet paper between her legs, she crept back to the bedroom to get her panties and then returned to the bathroom. She found some pads in the cupboard and some safety pins in a drawer. She pinned a pad to the crotch of her panties. Older sisters are good for something after all, she thought. Her belly felt as though it would drop out from between her legs, but at least her cramps had subsided. Back in the room she quietly put her pyjamas back on and slipped into bed.

When Nanny woke up the next morning, she saw that Billy had mysteriously retrieved her pyjamas, too. They got up, dressed in the usual way, with their backs to each other, and went outside to feed the horses. When Nanny pressed her lips to the velvet nose of her horse, she remembered the night before. She felt a stirring of anxiety. She didn't want anything to change. She glanced over at Billy, who grinned and said, "Nice fucking day for a ride, hey?"

"Fucking right," Nanny grinned back at her. "Let's pack some food and then ride over to the bluff."

Billy scooped out more oats with the plastic pail. "Good i-fucking-dea," she replied.

Flight

For Troy

CLICK. ANNA LOCKED the bathroom door. She could hear the TV in the next room. The familiar voice of Ed Sullivan accompanied her as she slipped the button and undid the side zipper of her stretchies. Good—they were all absorbed in the Sunday night ritual and wouldn't notice how long she was in there.

After peeling off her slacks, she hung them by the stirrups on the door knob. As she bent to remove her underpants, she saw the pale yellow stain on the crotch panel and wished for red. It was a vague wish with no hope in it. For days now she had closed her eyes and prayed for that dark smear on her panties. Over and over she had made promises to God. Please, God, if I see blood I will never…but what could she promise? What sins had she committed that were big enough to trade for the longed-for reprieve? She imagined that God was like her father—easily angered. If you bothered him or got in his way he would lash out and strike you down. She didn't consider praying to Mary. She imagined that Mary was like her mother—too busy.

She left the hopeless panties in a puddle on the tiled floor and stepped into the empty bathtub. She was cold. Even though she left her T-shirt and her sweater on, she felt exposed standing there naked from the waist down. She unscrewed the lid. (She wished she could be unscrewed…she was coming unscrewed, was coming loose, was already loose or she wouldn't be standing in a bathtub with a jar of mustard in her hands.) French's Mustard. It made her think of French kissing. She remembered the boy who had first put his tongue in her mouth and how she had thought it was like having a slug shoved down her throat. That invasion had some-how felt like more of a violation than having sex the first time. She was more familiar with her mouth than with her vagina—more accustomed to its desires and pleas-ures and she more clearly understood it as her own.

Anna put the lid on the side of the tub and spread her legs. (See, that's what you get for spreading your legs in the first place, she thought.) She scooped the mustard out with her fingers. It ran down her hand and forearm in gory yellow dribbles, slid slowly down her thin white thighs and fell in aborted plops and splats onto her bare feet. Her fingers felt the smooth tight walls of her vagina contract and expand as she struggled to get the stuff inside. She wrinkled her nose at the smell—it reminded her of hot dogs and her tummy felt queasy at the thought. Hoping to get more inside her, she squatted, but as she did, a stream of yellow gushed out. Her vagina felt as though it was burning and finally she ran the tap and rinsed the mustard off her inner lips and hands and legs. She prayed that some, enough, had stayed inside.

Anna had decided to try the mustard because she'd overheard her big sister's girlfriend saying that it could draw sperm out. Getting the jar, unnoticed, out of the fridge and into the bathroom had been quite a trick. She worried, too, about her mother missing it. Where can a brand-new jar of mustard go? *The Missing Mustard Mystery* by Nancy Drew. The thought made Anna smile a crooked half-smile. She felt as though she were standing on the edge of a precipice with a strong wind at her back and somehow that smile was saving her.

Anna wondered about a lot of things. Like why she didn't have a cherry. She'd heard the guys at school joke about popping cherries and she knew from talking to her sisters that once a cherry popped, it would bleed and that would mean the girl wasn't a virgin anymore. Anna really worried about her cherry. Where was it? What was wrong with her? She didn't bleed when he did it to her the first time. She had been expecting some pain—not much—and then some blood—just a little—and then the earth was supposed to move. Or at least that's what happened in the romantic pocket books she and her sisters read. What she felt at the time was nothing. No pain, no blood. Nothing, nothing, nothing. There was a feeling of pressure but that was familiar because he'd been poking at her for weeks, the blunt head blindly pounding at her door as though it were some kind of creature with a mind of its own.

Anna thought of her boyfriend's penis as his *thing*. The first time Anna saw it she was horrified. All raw purple ugliness, it had no redeeming features as far as she was concerned. Yet he seemed so proud of his penis, displayed it eagerly with a *ta da* look on his face. Anna was tactful, reached out and touched it gingerly. I can't let on how I feel about it, she thought. She knew she had to pretend she liked his penis and didn't pull her hand away when he showed her how to stroke it up and down. Weird how the skin moves over the hard center, she thought. Creepy.

When he pulled her head down and pushed his penis into her mouth, she gagged and felt certain that she would throw up. She tried to pull away, but he held her firmly there and then suddenly her mouth was filling up with sticky salty slime. She didn't know what it was and in a panic looked frantically around for a place to spit it out. Surely she wasn't expected to swallow it! She ran to the window and spat and spat, but the taste stayed and burned at the back of her throat. His feelings were hurt. From then on, Anna swallowed.

Their being together always ended up at the old boarded-up fishing cabin down by Painter's Lodge. Being there was boring. Anna wanted to have fun, *do* something. It was always his idea to go; Anna didn't like it there. The cabin was cobwebby and smelly and cold. At first she thought it was a cute little house—a cute little house all their own. It was usually night-time when they went to the cabin. Then one time they went there during the day and Anna thought, Oh God, this is really awful. She went later with a broom to clean up and felt a hopeful playing-house kind of feeling, but soon she was overwhelmed by the cobwebs and gave up. It was worse after that day because she'd seen it in the light. She found it helped if she closed her eyes.

One night after the show—Anna had finally talked him into *doing* something—he said, "Let's go down to the cabin for a quickie."

"It's kind of late, Don...I have to be home soon...you know what my dad's like."

"Aw, c'mon, Anna. I did what *you* wanted. How about a little give-and-take, huh?"

Anna didn't want to go. It was a windy night with a big moon and the trees on either side of the unlit highway were throwing great wild shadows around them as they walked. The movie they had just seen was *Hush, Hush, Sweet Charlotte* and Anna didn't feel like leaving the main road and walking down the spooky trail to the cabin.

"C'mon, Anna, it's on the way. You won't be very late. Just tell your dad it was a long movie."

Anna wanted to say no, but she just couldn't make herself say it. Don had stopped walking and he was standing with his arms folded and he had *that look* on his face. The next day was Saturday and she knew that if she didn't go along with him now, he'd sulk all day or go out drinking beer with his friends instead of seeing her.

"OK, I guess we can go for a little while," she said reluctantly. When they got to the cabin, they went straight to the mouldy little cot as usual and he climbed on top of her. God, she thought, he just humps away as though I'm not even here. Looking over his shoulder, she could see his hips pumping up and down. It made her think of dogs doing it. She closed her eyes. He had his fly open and his penis was out but he was on the outside of her panties so it seemed innocent enough. *Going all the way* didn't occur to her. She assumed he would ask—that it would be an occasion, that there would be some kind of discussion about it—and she would be in charge of making the decision about losing her virginity. She started thinking about losing her virginity. Where would it go? Could it be found again?

(You bad little kittens...You've lost your mittens...) Anna found herself smiling—that same little half-smile again, the one that made her feel like she was far away and separate from what was happening to her. She turned her face away so he wouldn't see. Not that he ever looks at me when he's doing this, she thought.

Oh God, she thought, this is *so* boring...and I am going to be *so* late and what am I going to tell my dad? She opened her eyes and looked up at the ceiling. The moonlight was coming through the grubby windows, illuminating all the cobwebs and reminding her of the possibility of spiders dropping. She was feeling squashed lying there between him and the damp mattress, but mostly she was just bored. He seems really into what he's doing...if I try to stop him now, he'll want to put his thing in my mouth. "C'mon," he'll say, "you've got to finish what you've started." Anna began to notice that he was pushing harder than usual and his breath was loud in her ear. Suddenly he stopped. He lay very still on top of her for a moment and then he said, "Oh God. I'm sorry, I'm sorry."

"What for?" This is really weird, she thought.

"I slipped in," he said.

Her hand of its own volition darted down. She could feel the base of his penis right up against her vagina. It felt strange to have a part of someone else inside her, to be joined like this. They were attached. The sensation of being attached was somehow romantic, but she also felt invaded. It felt creepy, like she was eating him or he was sticking into her...like a knife.

Anna said, "That's OK." She knew that's what you were supposed to say when guys said they were sorry. She sat up then and started to cry.

"Sorry, sorry, sorry," he kept saying.

"I'm not crying about that." She tried to explain. "I'm upset because I didn't feel anything. There must be something wrong with me. I'll have to tell my mother, see a doctor," she said between sobs.

He tried to reassure her. "Don't worry," he said, "we'll try again in a couple of days and maybe you'll feel something then."

Yes, Anna thought, maybe he's right. After all, he's had more experience with this than I have. Anna wasn't his first. It was all over school that the year before, he'd gotten a girl in trouble. Her name was Sandra. Anna had never met her but she had heard that Sandra had given the baby up for adoption.

That baby had been born only a few months before Anna met Don. Knowing this about him did not make Anna want to stay away from him. Instead, from the moment that she'd heard the gossip, she had felt drawn to him. He was a father! Now that was something. And his fatherhood was fresh—she could almost smell it on him.

When she looked at him or sat next to him, her body was gripped with an excitement that was so intense it was close to fear. Her heart would pound in her throat and her hands would break out in a sweat. She felt desperate about it. I just have to have him, she thought.

Anna had been the one to go after Don. She asked him to dance at the school sockhop. She knew he was too shy to ask her first, but after that he did. He didn't exactly ask her, but would catch her eye from across the room and jerk his head toward the dance floor. When he made that gesture, Anna felt a thrill run through her and a sharp pain in her heart that she thought was love. Oh God, she thought, he is so cool.

Within a couple of months they were spending all their time together and soon it was down to the old shack for the dry humping routine.

After that first time, they had sex again—to see if Anna could feel anything. The next few times she could, but it was just a thick fullness inside her. She felt stretched and achy afterwards. It seemed very important to tell him that it felt good, so she did. It also seemed imperative to do it whenever he wanted, which was all the time. He would get so desperate. Every time they were alone, and as soon as they kissed, he would want to do it. Anna felt as though it was her fault that he got so turned on. He would put her hand on the front of his jeans and she could feel his penis straining to get out. She imagined that she could hear it whining, "Let me out, let me out..." When he opened his fly, his penis would spring out at her and bob around on his belly. The skin was stretched smooth and tight over the engorged head and what looked like a drop of spittle oozed out of the little mouth. Protruding blue veins pulsed up the erect shaft. It looked so eager and demanding. Like an angry little soldier. Anna had the feeling each time that she had created some kind of monster and now she had to feed it.

Don never touched her, not even her breasts, with his hands—as though he was only interested in her from the waist down. Anna felt sad about this when she found out she was pregnant. How can I be pregnant when my breasts are still virgins? she thought. It all seemed somehow out of order and upside down.

Anna knew she was pregnant before she missed a period. She just had a strong feeling about it. She went to her doctor. At first he refused to do a test. She cried and repeated over and over, "I just know I am." Finally he tested her and said he'd call her in about a week with the results.

"Oh no," she pleaded, "don't call my house. I don't want my parents to know." The doctor agreed to let her call him and said that he'd keep it a secret for a while. He assured her that she would probably start her period before the test came back. I know different, she thought. I just know.

Anna called the doctor from a phone booth beside the bus stop the next week. From where she stood, she could see her friends sitting in the café having cokes and she felt conspicuous in the phone booth. As though anyone using a phone booth was surely pregnant.

"The test is positive," the doctor said. Positive, Anna thought. It sounded like good news. She put her hand over her tummy. A baby, I'm going to have a baby! The words washed over her, bringing a warm rush.

"OK, uh, thanks," Anna said and pushed the disconnect button with her finger, keeping the receiver to her ear as though she were still talking. She wasn't ready to step out of the booth yet and rejoin her friends. Oh God, she thought. Oh God, oh God, oh God... She hung her head so that her hair covered her face. She felt confused and as the enormity of her situation began to sink in, the warmth left her and was followed by dread. As though a slow dark substance was moving through her veins. She slumped against the wall. No, she thought. No. A baby—a little baby all my own. But she felt split open, spilled out all over. As though her insides had fallen out. A bloody mess, she thought. And no one to clean it up but me.

Anna grasped desperately for something to hold onto, but it was like falling in the dark. As though she had been pushed over the edge of a deep chasm with no hope of wings. Nothing to save her. And her body felt rigid with fear, as though she were falling and falling and waiting for the ground to hit.

Anna pressed her forehead hard against the window of the phone booth and the hard glass helped to clear her mind. She squeezed her eyes shut to stay the tears. Taking a deep breath, she tossed her hair back from her face and put the receiver back in its cradle. As she stepped out of the phone booth, she wrapped her arms around herself, but she couldn't feel anybody there.

For the first four months, Anna carried the restless secret in her belly hidden under big shirts. Her tummy swelled a little, but no one noticed—they were all wearing their fathers' oversize shirts that year. Her breasts grew. That was OK. Her sisters were envious of her new bustline. In Home Ec class, she made herself a dress. The material was navy blue with a maroon paisley pattern—big fat tear drops splashed all over. The style she chose was an empress line and she stitched on a wide blue velvet ribbon which tied in a bow right under her breasts. The scoop neck showed her new cleavage and the wide skirt hid the small mound of tummy. She got an A from her teacher and wore the dress for her sixteenth birthday party.

On the day of her party, she set her hair in her mother's wire brush rollers. Her hair was long and her arms ached by the time she had the last of the sections rolled and stuck securely with the little pink plastic stick pins. She wrapped her head in a pink chiffon kerchief, tied it at the back and went downtown to shop for new nylons and a blue velvet ribbon to tie in her hair. She also bought a new lipstick—Palest Peach. When she reached home, she struggled with getting the rollers out—that really hurt. Some of them were so tangled in her hair that she had to rip them out. Then she backcombed the top section, pinned it under at the back and placed the new bow just right. She combed out the rest of her hair into a perfect flip. On her lids she put pale blue eyeshadow and over each eye she applied peel-off black liner which she artfully turned up at the corners. Then she put on her new dress and stood in front of the mirror. She thought she looked pretty. She didn't feel pregnant at all.

One day shortly after her birthday party, Anna felt a soft stroking on the inside of her tummy. The life there saying hello. Hi. I'm here. She cupped her hand gently over her belly and closed her eyes. She was listening with her whole body and it was as though she could hear a small voice singing. She sensed a darkness in there too, though, and it glowered and threatened. Anna imagined the darkness retreating to a small corner of her mind to brood and plot. "You're not finished with me yet," it muttered. Just like the bad guy in the comics, she thought. She knew he'd be back.

By Anna's fifth month, she began to show. She ballooned and ballooned and the soft paintbrush strokes that had tickled her on the inside became easy rolls. It reminded her of the feeling of her tongue rolling on the inside of her cheek. In the following months, blunt elbows and knees began to poke at her and little feet caught under her ribs.

Her breasts became unrecognizable—enormous and blue-veined with large chocolate-brown areolas and erect nipples that rubbed painfully on her stiff cotton brassiere. Her tummy pushed ever more determinedly out of her skirts, prying the zippers open, and was finally uncontainable. "Look at me, look at me!" It shouted itself out of all of her clothes. "Shhh..." she wanted to say.

By September, the clothes she had bought in August no longer fit her. At school, no one would talk to her or sit with her at lunch—not even Don. He seemed embarrassed, ashamed of her. So she sat alone on the curb out by the parking lot and opening her little brown bag, ate the peanut butter sandwiches and the Dad's Cookies and then waited for the bell, with her sweater tugged down and her arms folded over her swollen belly. Anna loved school and dreaded quitting. Quitting school felt like dying, but those long lunch hours on the curb were unbearable and she finally gave in— one day she just stopped going. For the rest of that term she stayed home a lot and continued to do *his* home- work—she'd been doing this since shortly after she'd met him—so that he could graduate. She didn't com- plain; she loved writing the essays and devoured the penned-in comments from his teachers when they were returned. Those red-inked words of praise were her lifelines to the real world.

When Anna's time came and the waters gushed out

of her like all the unshed tears of the past months, she phoned her mother. She wanted her mother. Then the pains began like whines and became hot cries that burned into her from the inside out. Like screams from the underworld. Persistent and sharp-edged, the pains tore through her over and over again. Each one would build and crest and then recede, leaving less and less time in-between. Wave after wave after wave. Anna could hear herself whimpering, "Oh no, not again..." each time another one began. She was no longer herself. She was a grunting, panting animal writhing on the sheets. In the brief moments between the peaks, she looked frantically around for her mother. She was afraid of the darkness behind the pain. The darkness called to her in an evil and seductive voice. "I told you I'd be back," it said. "Now come to me, my little pretty..." When she saw her mother leaving, she wanted to cry out, beg her to stay. *(Please don't go, Mom...I'm afraid of the dark...)* Then there was only the pain and she clung to the waves and rode them in and rode them out oblivious to anything but the struggle not to go under.

Sixteen hours passed. The day gave way to night and the pain gave way to a pressure that built and built. It was as though she were expanding until she filled the whole room. She felt she would explode, be ripped open. She was. The doctor was late—no time for a neat cut—and the tearing was a white-hot burn drowned by a warm gush as a fish-slippery child slid out of her body.

They handed her an enormous baby *(I made this?)* wrapped doll-fashion in rough blue terry. A boy. *(What will I do with a boy? It was supposed to be a girl—like me. It looks like him.)* Anna could hear the click-click-click of the blakeys on Don's Fry boots as he paced just outside the door of the delivery room.

The doctor was stitching her up but it was a sensation far away. She was absorbed by the gum-pink round face with the black almond eyes. She wanted to eat him. Lick and bite and swallow him back into her. The hot blood flowed between her legs and her nipples burned. Anna felt tears brimming and then spilling over as she looked down at her baby, but she didn't feel sad. She felt something more powerful than she'd ever felt before. It was as though her heart had cracked open and all of her was pouring out. As though her whole being was reaching out and wrapping itself around this little creature. She was suddenly aware of his fragility. She buried her face in the folds of his neck, felt the damp hair against her face. He smelled like sweet earth. He's so new, she thought. Newer than a brand-new doll at Christmas. Mixed with this tenderness was another feeling. It was as though the hair bristled at the back of her neck and her teeth had become long and sharp.

Then they took the baby away. *(Where? Where?)* They told Don to go home—he didn't object. The nurse told her that she was tired now. *(I am not tired, not at all.)* She put Anna in a room and left her there alone. Far into the night, wide-eyed Anna yearned. She was utterly empty, she had nothing left, not even herself *(Who am I?)*.

Early the next morning, they brought her the blue terry bundle and told her to wait, that someone would come and show her how to feed him. He was crying and she didn't wait. She knew how to do this. The knowing was in her body—like breathing. When they came back he was asleep on her belly—they were both naked and asleep. They woke her and scolded her and dressed him and took him away. A punishment.

Five days later, they let Anna take the baby home. Home for Anna was a basement suite. It was dark. It was a dark time. She was a shadow moving through her own life. There were small bright bubbles of time when she was in communion with her baby, their faces inches apart while she changed, bathed and fed him. They were in their own little world.

The rest of the time, Anna felt desperately unhappy. She knew she didn't love Don. What's wrong with me, she thought. He's a good person—it's not like he beats me. He's not mean to me—well, not intentionally mean. Sometimes he said things to Anna that she felt she'd never get over.

"My God, what happened to you?" he said one day. He was referring to her breasts after she'd stopped breast-feeding. Once the milk dried up, her breasts were like empty vessels, blue-lined and stretched painfully thin. Her little nubile breasts hadn't had a chance to assert themselves before she got pregnant. They were wiped out. She couldn't remember what they'd looked like. His words cut deep and from then on Anna carried her breasts like wounds.

But Anna knew that Don loved her. Deep down he's really a good person, she kept telling herself.

"What are you...stupid?" he'd say sometimes. Anna felt bad inside whenever he said this. Maybe I really am stupid, she thought. But even more than the words was the way he had of looking at her, rolling his eyes back and grunting his disapproval.

Anna knew this was the way men were supposed to treat their wives. At least Don helps me with the dishes, she thought (even though she was instructed not to tell anyone that he did this). I shouldn't be so sensitive. They're just harmless remarks. They were remarks about her stupidity usually, or her inability to organize her life to the expected perfection. It was well-known in Don's family that Anna was not succeeding as a housewife.

That year was a blur of diapers, the wringer washer, the housework, the pressure to have dinner on time. Anna couldn't do it. She hadn't been trained for it. She'd grown up in the back of a store and worked in the café, pumped gas, did dishes, made chips and burgers. It had never occurred to her to sweep under a bed. She didn't know what dusting was, had never heard of it. She liked to cook but the organization part was beyond her. She liked to create, experiment with food. All Don would eat was meat and potatoes, carrots and corn. Period. Every night, five o'clock on the dot. He would come home from school at four o'clock, sit in front of the TV and watch "Star Trek" until dinner. It's not as though he yells and swears at me if dinner isn't ready, she thought. What got to her was the snort and that dismissive look. Always followed by the slow shake of his head. It made her feel like she was disappearing. Every time he did it, she felt smaller and smaller until she imagined that one day she would just be a crumb on the floor. After dinner, he'd go out with his buddies and come home late, smelling of beer. Anna would clean up and put the baby to bed and then do Don's homework. If she wasn't already asleep when he came in, she pretended she was. He would usually wake her up to *do it* anyway. He often bragged about how envious his friends were that he got some *tail* every night.

Anna began having dreams about jumping out of windows. Not falling. Flying. In the morning, after one of these dreams, she looked out the window of the basement suite and saw the small spring crocuses pushing out of the soil right there, at eye level, and she felt utterly hopeless. There was nowhere to go, no beautiful free space for her wings to unfurl and carry her through. To escape, she would have had to crawl out on her hands and knees.

One day, Anna looked around the kitchen. It was almost dinnertime and she had prepared nothing. He would be home soon. The house must be clean, the food ready. She knew the rules. (She bent them a little sometimes. Unrolled the sleeves of yesterday's shirts, ironed them and hung them in the closet. Bought pre-cooked, barbecued chickens from the corner store and pulled them out of the cold oven at five o'clock.)

She knew she must go to the store now, buy something for dinner. She bundled up the sleeping baby, picked up her purse and walked out the door. She walked down the familiar street to the corner grocery and she found herself walking right by. With every step she felt the weight of her body leaving her. She could no longer feel the earth beneath her feet. She felt a rush of wind in her face and she imagined she could hear great wings beating in her ears. She kept on walking and never went back. Not ever.

Sweetheart

For Dave

ANNA'S FIRST DATE after she left Don was with a guy she'd met a few months before. A friend of Don's. He was older and had introduced them to acid and pot. Don thought he was the greatest. Anna did too. She felt all melty around him because one day he'd called her sweetheart.

"Go get me some cigarettes willya, sweetheart?"

No one had ever called her sweetheart before. The most she usually ever heard from Don was a grunt. The same grunt could mean "Yes" or "No" or "I just came."

Rick—that was his name—was twenty-eight. Anna had just turned seventeen.

About a month after Anna left Don, she received a phone call from Rick. He wanted to take her to Victoria for the day. Anna had never been on a date before—not a real one. When she'd started going out with Don, they'd just kind of hung out. Rick had a car. He made lots of money in the logging camps and would probably take her out to dinner, she thought.

To be taken out to dinner was to be treated like a princess. Anna chose her best skirt—the one with the lovely swirls of purple paisley. She had bought the skirt last fall. She'd known that it wouldn't fit her around the waist by the time school started but she'd bought it anyway, and worn it with the zipper half-undone and her sweater pulled determinedly down over top. The skirt hadn't fit for the first six months after she'd had the baby either, but it fit now. She passed her hands lovingly over the smooth fabric and stood up on tiptoe in front of the small mirror to check that her blouse was tucked in evenly all around.

Clothes were important to Anna. She liked things to match and she liked them to be just right. She bent and tugged at her nylons. They were new, with no nail polish blobs obstructing the course of the runs that usually streaked up from her ankles. Like stretch marks, Anna thought, and then her mind darted away. Now was not a good time to think about those raw blue-and-red tracks that raced over her hips, belly and breasts like the trail of some whirling demon. She dreamed once that the creature from the "Tasmanian Devil" cartoon she'd watched as a child had visited her in the night and burned his passage onto her skin. Her body had been different before the baby. Her skin had stretched smooth and taut over her bones. A clean page.

As she adjusted her garters and dropped her skirt, she thought about dinner. She wondered what they would have. Where they would eat. She hoped she wouldn't seem too young to Rick, and not know what to order. Maybe it would be best to let him order for her? As she thought about how delicious the food would be, her tummy tightened in anticipation. Anna loved food and could eat lots. She'd always had a big appetite and was proud of it—it was a way of showing off. People would say: "My, my, look how much she can put away, and such a little thing too!"

One time, though, when Anna was a little girl, her aunt had shamed her for eating so many pancakes at breakfast. This same aunt had later called Anna a slut. She'd said Anna was boy-crazy when she and her cousin stole a Boysenberry Pie sign from a restaurant. Anna and her cousin were only twelve—they thought the sign was funny because it had the word *boys* in it. Somehow the pancake incident and the slut incident had become mixed up in Anna's mind. When she remembered them, her tummy tightened again, but this time with an unpleasant twist. She resolved to eat delicate little bites of her food and leave some on her plate no matter how hungry she was. Like a princess. Yes.

Maybe she'd better eat something now before he arrived? She hadn't had breakfast and it was almost lunchtime. No, she would wait. She would save her appetite and everything would taste extra delicious. Anyway, he would be there any minute. Her tummy felt fluttery and light. She couldn't imagine putting anything in it and anyway, eating might give her bad breath. She brushed her teeth once more just in case and then reapplied her lipstick—Palest Peach. "Ugh, you look like a corpse with that white stuff on your lips!" her father would say. She didn't care. What did he know?

Living at home again with my parents feels weird, Anna thought. I'm grown-up now. I have my own baby, after all, and they can't boss me around the way they used to. Her father didn't dare hit her anymore but the looks he gave her made her feel dirty. Anna's mother seemed to resent having her around—as though she'd been relieved to finally get rid of one child and was dismayed when a year later, she got two back. She was good about helping with the baby, though, and had agreed to take him for the day.

By the time Rick arrived, Anna felt all glowy and the word *sweetheart* was humming in her head like a warm purr.

During the ninety-minute ride to Victoria, Anna felt pleased with herself and grown-up. She chatted about anything that came into her head and, aside from the little worry nibbling at her that he would find her boring and not mature enough, she was having a lovely time. Rick didn't say much on the drive—only reached over from time to time and gave her knee a squeeze. This seemed OK to Anna. The radio played: "Bend me, shape me, any way you want me...As long as you love me it's alright..." Anna thought, Isn't this just the best song? but she didn't dare say it out loud. What if Rick didn't like the song or thought it was babyish...she would just die.

As soon as they reached the outskirts of Victoria, Anna felt the thrill of the big city wash over her, but Rick turned right and drove along a winding road that was taking them away from the city. Before Anna had a chance to ask where they were going, he turned into a parking lot. Sans Souci Motel, the sign said. Anna's worry about not being mature enough turned from a nibbling into a gnawing. She looked up at him. He was looking at her and smiling. It was a hungry smile.

"Now you just wait right here, sweetheart, and I'll be right back," he said. He was in charge. He knew what he was doing. Anna felt as though an ancient signal in her body had begun to change her from skin and bone to a more malleable substance. Something soft and fluffy and timid. She felt it first in her face as she returned his smile. Her cheeks plumped out like bread dough. The skin around her eyes followed the upward curve of her putty lips with acquiescent crinkles.

"OK," she said. Her eyes dropped to the pattern on her skirt. She traced each fat teardrop shape carefully with her finger. The late October sun shone coolly on her lap, making the colours bright.

While he was gone, she felt an overwhelming desire to run. Her legs twitched and her breath came in shallow gasps, but a voice deep inside whispered: "Don't move, little rabbit." Anna shivered and the hair prickled on the back of her neck. The paisleys blurred. Rick came back to the car.

"So, we're all set...Mrs. Smith!" His grin was sharp. Anna could see his teeth gleaming at her wetly. Somehow she got her body out of the car. She caught the glint of metal in his hand as they approached the motel room door. She was mesmerized by the key fumbling briefly at the hole and then sliding smoothly in with a quick twist. She felt it, that twist, in the bottom of her womb like a sharp pinched *No!* The door swung wide and she felt as though she were falling. His hand was at her back, just at that vulnerable place below the rib cage, where there is no resistance.

He guided her gently toward the bed. Roughly, and she would have fought him off. On her shoulder, and she would have shrugged him off. "Wait a minute! You can't make me do this!" she would have said. On her bum, and she would have said: "Hold it right there, buddy. No one treats me like that!" But that in-between place on her back was open and full of fear and his sweaty hand had her there where she had no defence. His hand pushed her forward effortlessly, as a strong wind would bend a small tree to the ground.

Anna sat on the edge of the bed with her smile frozen on her face. It was as though she were made of putty; having been pressed up against him, she had become an imprint. A picture of his desire. His need. A chameleon-like state with a macabre twist. To transform according to his desire. To be desired. To be chosen. To be taken. To be devoured.

Rick went into the bathroom. Anna listened with horror to the long stream of his pee and flinched in spasms of shame at the two squirts she heard at the end. She didn't want to know this about him. Princes didn't pee. They didn't even have penises. She didn't hear the water run in the sink so she knew he hadn't washed his hands. He came out and pulled her up off the bed; she cringed as his hand touched hers.

"Now you go in there and have a wash," he said, and gave her a small push toward the bathroom.

Anna closed the bathroom door. Wash. He must mean *down there.* Did he think she wasn't clean? She realized with a clutch of anxiety that she didn't know which underwear she had on. Oh God, please let them be my good ones, she prayed as she hiked up her skirt. Looking down she saw they were her good ones. It was a huge relief.

Anna put the hem of her skirt in her teeth and pulled her panties down around her knees. A pale yellow stain on the white cotton panel. Dry. She took a frayed washcloth from the stack of towels on the shelf above the toilet, held it under the tap, and began to wash herself. The more she washed, the dirtier she felt inside. She rubbed the rough cloth hard over the soft pink skin but she couldn't feel anything much. Just numb rubbing. She looked up at herself briefly in the mirror over the sink and saw her brown eyes look vacantly back.

Anna came out of the bathroom. Rick was lying naked on the bed. She stood frozen and could not bring herself to look at Rick. Her gaze darted wildly from the floor to the ceiling, from the window to the door. Anna found herself thinking about the time a sparrow had accidentally flown in her bedroom window. She remembered how the trapped bird had flown desperately around and around, finally flying into one of the window panes. It had died.

"Come here." His voice was sure, commanding.

Anna stepped toward the bed, then turned quickly around to sit perched on its edge. She bent to take her shoes off and felt his hands working at the button of her skirt and then tugging at the zipper. She began to concentrate hard on sliding out each of the small rubber nubs of her garters. Reaching around with both hands to the hooks and eyes at the back of her garter belt, she unclasped them quickly and pulled the belt off. She slipped it out from under her skirt and onto the floor. The belt was grey and shabby and one of the elastic straps was held on with a safety pin. She pushed it under the bed with one foot.

"C'mon baby, Peter can't wait all day."

Rick was close behind her now and pushing his *peter* into the small of her back. She moved close to the edge of the bed, unrolled her nylons, and peeled them off. He slid her panties down her bum and pulling her onto her back, tugged them down her legs and off her feet. She kept her legs close together and averted her face as he climbed on top of her and began grunting and poking at her. His penis, she noticed, was small. Much smaller than Don's. It made her think of the word *dink* and the boy's penis she saw once when she was twelve. She and the boy were in the same class. She had dared him to show her and he had. When he dared her back she had run away.

Her blouse was still buttoned to the top and she was glad. She felt very shy about her breasts, especially after the baby. Rick didn't seem to notice anything about her from the waist up. No kissing or groping. Just the single-minded poking between her legs.

"Open up, sweetheart. C'mon, let me in..." He said this impatiently and Anna felt hurt, but she opened her legs slightly. With one quick jab he was in.

Anna stared hard at the wall. She followed the pattern of the wallpaper, looking for faces and animal shapes, but his moving blurred the lines. Her gaze left the wall, flashed past the window and focused on the bedside table near her face. Under the tilted lampshade she could see the light bulb and she looked right into it until her eyes burned. Then she shut them and watched the starbursts behind her closed lids.

Something was wrong. Rick kept pumping and pumping. He was taking too long. His breathing sounded frustrated and angry. He brought his mouth close to her ear and whispered: "Say *fuck me—fuck me*. C'mon baby, say it."

"I can't." Anna felt sick. She'd never said *fuck* in front of a man before. She and her best friend Wilamena used to play tough and say it to each other, but she couldn't imagine saying it to Rick.

"Don't be a baby. C'mon, it turns me on. Do it. Say it. C'mon, I need you to say it."

He was still moving inside her, but Anna couldn't feel much. His penis seemed to be sliding in and out, but there was no friction, barely any contact with the walls of her vagina.

Anna kept her eyes shut and said nothing. She felt humiliation creep up her body and wrap itself around her whole being. She knew it was her fault. Her vagina was too big from having the baby. She tried to squeeze herself tighter inside and moved her hips a little to help.

"Yeah baby, that's it, now c'mon, say it..."

Anna tried making some small sounds and breathed

harder, the way she used to do with Don—that whole year they were together—to hurry things up. (Afterwards, she would go into the bathroom and make herself come.)

Suddenly, Rick stopped and pulled away. Anna felt exposed and drew her legs together. She felt panicky. She knew he hadn't come. She knew it was her fault. She knew then that no other man would ever want her.

Rick made a disgusted sound and grabbed Anna by the hips, turning her in one brutal motion onto her stomach. Before she knew what was happening, he was pushing at her from behind. She wriggled up trying to accommodate him but he stayed right where he was. He was pushing at the wrong hole! Anna squeezed her eyes and her fists and her anus as tight as she could and squirmed up on the bed. Her elbows were bent underneath her chest and her hands clutched at the bed sheets trying to pull away. Her head was butting up against the wall, her neck scrunched into her shoulders, and still he rammed into her. She couldn't keep him out. His big hands dug into her hips as he pounded away.

It hurt. She was terrified that she was going to shit—wasn't sure that she hadn't already—couldn't tell what was happening to her and she burned with hot sticky shame.

She knew it was her fault.

When he finally stopped, he pulled out fast and disappeared into the bathroom without a word.

Anna's anus was burning. Anna's vagina was rejected. Simply inadequate.

She curled up, pulling her knees under her and burying her face in her hands. She heard water running in the bathroom and she knew he was washing. Washing her off.

When he came out of the bathroom, he was in a hurry. Anna was still putting on her nylons and she desperately wanted to wash.

"C'mon, sweetheart, let's split."

The long ride home was quiet except for Rick's whistling. The same tune over and over: "Bend me, shape me..."

Anna sat with her face slightly averted and studied the frost patterns on the window. It had been a cold day. She was hungry.

Cookie

For all the "tough cookies" out there

THE SEINER WAS ANCHORED in the San Juan Straits in swells that obliterated the horizon and made it necessary for the crew to hook themselves to a rope to piss overboard. It was a well-known fact that the majority of fishermen drowned were found with their flies open, the inevitable result of too much alcohol and a rough sea.

This was Anna's first summer on a fish boat and it was her dream come true. She'd grown up in a little fishing village on Vancouver Island and all her life she'd heard about making big bucks on the boats, especially on the purse seiners. The seiners didn't have to troll along waiting for the fish to bite. Like giant spiders, they spun out their nets from a big spool at the back and waited for the salmon to swim in. Each set was out for about an hour and then the crew would reel the net in, pulling the ends together like a huge drawstring purse, and dump the catch on deck. They never knew what they would net but if the salmon were running, one set could be worth thousands of dollars. Oh, how she'd envied the boys who went out each summer and came back flashing the dough. Of course it was always the boys. They got all the breaks. They even got hired on as cooks. What did they know about cooking?

Anna left her home town when she was sixteen, taking her young son with her, and she'd been living in the big city of Vancouver ever since. She'd worked as a short-order cook and waitress until she was sick of peeling potatoes and peeling the men's hands off her young body. Often, in her dreams, the hands came at her—faceless, bodiless hands touching, kneading, clawing, grasping and grabbing at her.

After Anna left school, her biggest goal was to get off welfare. When she first got to Vancouver, she put herself through secretarial school. Drumming away at a typewriter made the tips of her fingers numb; the deadness crept up her arms and spread throughout her entire being. She felt she would die of boredom if she had to work at a job like that, and she knew the men's hands would be there too. At twenty-two, Anna signed up for some psychology and English literature classes at the local college. Then she discovered that she couldn't go back to school without getting kicked off Social Assistance.

"You mean you'll support me as long as I stay home and do nothing but you'll cut my funds if I try to get an education so I can support myself?" Anna was incredulous. It seemed to her that the social worker was looking down his nose at her and thinking: If you hadn't been such a little slut you wouldn't be in this position to start with. She couldn't believe that the welfare system worked like that—it was as though they wanted to keep her poor. Fuck you, she thought, and sneaked in a couple of courses here and there. Life was tough but so was Anna. She got a night job as a ballroom dance instructor. They trained her for free and it was fun learning the dances. Especially the cha-cha. Of course she had to deal with the hands. They slid insidiously onto her bum and brushed up against her breasts but she was resigned to it. She learned quickly that the only jobs available to her were the ones she could get with a pretty face. To Anna, her beauty was a curse; it seemed all the wrong doors opened for her because of it.

Anna spent the rest of her time shuffling her kid back and forth between sitters. She was lucky because her cousin lived nearby and babysat for free when Anna worked nights. She had so little time to spend with her son that a constant feeling of guilt crawled like spiders in her belly. Every now and then she'd think: If only I could get a job on a fish boat—just one summer and I could make enough money to go back to school full-time. Then I could get a good job teaching school. Or maybe I could be a child psychologist. Dreams.

The summer she turned twenty-five, she received a phone call from her former boyfriend, her son's father. He kept in touch and sent money when he could and saw his son on holidays.

"There's a job on a boat," he said. "The skipper is a real asshole, but he needs a cook right away—like tomorrowmorning—and his boat is docked in Steveston. He has to leave first thing in the morning or they'll miss the big run up the San Juan Straits. Do you think you can handle it? It'll be tough—the guy's a real jerk and it's a drinkin' crew."

"Fine, what time? Where do I have to be?"

Anna packed her bag and dropped her son off at her cousin's house that night.

All the way down to the dock Anna kept telling herself that she could handle the job. She'd be cooking for a crew of five—no big deal. Her family had owned a café and she'd been cooking since she was eleven years old. Why did she suddenly feel as though she didn't know the first thing about frying eggs? She would have to do all the shopping and clean-up too. I'm not afraid of hard work so why do I feel so damn nervous? she thought. It was the guys. Five guys makes ten hands and she knew what *they* were like. She'd grown up with guys like that. I can handle them, she thought. I'm different now, stronger. I'll work my butt off and cook the best damn meals they ever had and I'll do other jobs too. I'll pull in the nets and sort fish, whatever it takes.

When Anna arrived at the Steveston wharf, she set her jaw, pulled back her shoulders, and strode down the dock toward the *Coho Queen*. The boat was grinding up against the buffers attached to the pilings. The friction made an eerie, whining noise that sent shivers down Anna's spine.

"Hi," she said brightly, "I'm Anna, your new cook." She had steeled herself for whistles and half-cocked smiles and sliding eyes. She was used to that, but she was not prepared for the hard, cold stares that greeted her from the deck of the *Coho Queen*.

"So, start cookin'!" a particularly hairy specimen growled at her. His eyes did not meet hers even for a second. "We haven't had breakfast yet and we're pullin' outa here within an hour."

Anna blanched. She was used to people liking her, brightening up a little when they met her.

"Oh lighten up, ya dumb fuck," snapped a man on her left. His eyes, which were close-set and bloodshot, seemed from a small distance to colour co-ordinate with the shock of red hair sticking out in tufts all over his big head.

"Welcome aboard the *Coho*, little lady," he said,

making a sweeping gesture of mock gallantry toward the boat.

As much as Anna cringed at the title, she felt a rush of relief at his attempt at kindness. A moment later, her relief was replaced with a flood of humiliation when he looked side-long at his buddies and then sneered at her, "And now get to fuckin' cookin' before we get hungry enough to eat pussy for breakfast!" The crew's har-har-hars resounded across the water as she stepped down onto the deck, keeping a good-natured half-smile painted on her face. She was breathing hard and saying over and over to herself, I can handle this.

They travelled all that day and into the night at full throttle. The Georgia Strait was choppy; Anna added, "I won't be sick, I won't be sick..." to her determined, "I can handle this..." and chanted it over and over as she went back and forth from the roast in the oven to the open porthole where she sucked in the black sea air in desperate gulps.

It was almost midnight before Anna finished clean-up and she had to be up before dawn to start breakfast. Her sleep that night was punctuated by the snores of the men around her. The pitching of the boat rolled her back and forth in the narrow bunk. Everything smelled of engine oil and fish.

At four o'clock, a big foot pushed Anna awake, and the joker from the day before snarled, "Time to get up, princess." He was the *Coho*'s skipper and the crew called him Big Red. Anna leapt out of bed and pulled her jeans on in the dark. Pulling her hair back in an untidy pony-tail she stepped over the sill into the galley. She made eggs and bacon and toast. The men came and ate and headed out on deck. Not a word of thanks or good morning or how did you sleep. She'd soon learn not to expect any niceties and be grateful for the silence.

The second morning the guy they called Buck took one look at his eggs and said, "What is this shit? These eggs are cold as a nun's tit." He got up, stepped outside and tossed them overboard. With self-satisfied snickers the rest of the crew followed suit. Then they all sat back down around the table, thumping and cursing until she had placed fresh pairs of eggs on their plates. Anna ignored their jeers and said nothing, but she was appalled at the senseless waste. The insides of her cheeks were raw from where she had bitten down to keep her cool. It'll get better, she told herself. They're just testing me.

So went that night's salad with tangerines and al-monds and the chicken-and-avocado omelets the morn-ing after.

"We don't want no fuckin' gourmet food, Cookie," they said, so it was meat and potatoes, bacon and eggs, and white-bread sandwiches for lunch. Fine, she thought. Fine. Her hopes of softening them with good food were dashed in those first few days. Her attempts at using humour were equally hopeless. When she tried joking with the men or using wit to fend them off, they would snort and look side-long at each other as though there was always a bigger joke that Anna didn't get. The joke was always on her. As much as she tried to shield herself, their remarks bit deep and their coarse laughter resonated in her bones.

One blazing afternoon in a dead calm sea, Anna was baking dinner pies when Red walked into the galley. The crew probably didn't know the difference between home-baked and store-bought, but Anna liked to bake and no one had complained about her desserts yet. She was standing in front of the open oven door with the top half of the galley door swung wide in hopes of a breeze. The heat from the oven blared out at her. She was wearing a sleeveless T-shirt and the perspiration ran in steady trickles from under her arms and the creases beneath her breasts. She usually wore an over-shirt to keep the guys' eyes off her but today the heat was just too much.

As Anna turned from the stove with a hot pie in either hand she found herself face-to-face with Big Red. He wore a big grin and he stood so close she could see the sweat running through the curly hair on his chest. Anna was at eye level with his fleshy pink nipples. His skin beneath the hair was sunburned and freckled and his belly oozed out of his low-slung jeans. Anna laughed nervously and tried to move around him to the counter. The heat from the pies began to seep through the potholders as he side-stepped to block her way. Before she could say a word, his hands shot out and grabbed her nipples, pinching and twisting hard. Pain seared through her. She gasped and squeezed her eyes shut; by the time she opened them again he was on his way out the door. The pies hit the counter and slid back to the wall as Anna's hands flew to her breasts, which still burned painfully. Then in two strides she was out the door and onto the ship's deck. Rushing up behind Big Red, she pushed him hard on the back, and sent him lurching forward to the ship's rail.

"Hey!" she yelled, "don't you try that again—ever!"

Big Red recovered his balance and stared at her, unable to mask his surprise.

"Cool out, Cookie," he said with a tight grin. "What do you expect, wearin' almost nuthin' with yer tits stickin' out like that?"

"Just don't ever touch me again," Anna repeated and stared him down.

"Yeah, well, get back to work, little Miss Queen of Sheba," he spat, and climbed the ladder to the upper deck where the rest of the guys had gathered and were doing their har-har-har number.

Anna knew he'd really have it in for her now. The crew had been laughing at him as much as at her this time. Oh shit, she thought, now I've really blown it. Why couldn't I just keep my cool? Oh shit! She had a hard time keeping the tears back as she cleaned up, but by the time she finished she had them under control. She knew she couldn't cry—that would be the end of her—and resolved that there was no way she'd let them get to her like that again. Were they even human? They swore and grunted and farted and sucked on beer bottles from morning to night. The beer bottles were everywhere, trails of brown lumps all over the docks and beaches like the spoor of some great beast that had passed in the night. When the guys communicated, they did so in monosyllables. They appeared to Anna to be some foreign, carnivorous sub-species.

The night they arrived in the San Juan Straits the swells started and the *Coho Queen* sat like a small duck in a big sea. At first Anna was terrified. Soon enough she didn't have time to be afraid. As the boat lurched and rolled on waves that obliterated the horizon, she had to take little running steps back and forth just to keep her balance. Bracing herself every moment on counters and table tops, she frantically tried to prepare the food. The carrots went skidding across the chopping block as soon as they were cut and the juice from the roast in the oven hissed dramatically as it slopped over the sides of the shallow pan. She had to make sure the cupboard doors were latched shut or there would be heavy dishes and canned goods hurtling through the air into her face. Anna took out the glasses, steadied them on the counter, then looked inside the fridge for the milk, removing a flat of eggs to get at it. She put the eggs on the counter, quickly put the carton of milk down and reached to catch a glass that was sliding toward the edge. In that moment the eggs went flying and the half-gallon of milk hit the floor. The white liquid sloshed out but when Anna lunged for the carton, it was already on its way to the other side. It was soon empty and she gave up the pursuit. She started picking up egg shells and trying to mop up the mess, which ran away from her and then came flying back with the rock and roll of the boat. It was hopeless and finally, she couldn't stop the tears.

The skiff-man, a young fellow named Ed, stepped down into the galley. Don't start in on me, Anna thought. Just when she was sure he'd start teasing her about crying, he knelt down and began helping her clean up.

"Don't worry about it," he said gruffly. "Happens all'a time. Listen, I know the guys are giving you a hard time. They're a bunch of assholes. Don't let 'em get to you."

Once the mess was cleaned up, Ed gave her a few tips about how to handle the swells.

"I used to cook on a boat," he said. "I know what it's like down here. The guys are just pissed off because you're gettin' an equal cut and they don't think it's worth it—especially 'cause you're a chick."

Anna was grateful beyond reason for his support.

Finally, the *Coho Queen* left the San Juan Straits and headed back around the tip of Vancouver Island, cruising up the coast to dock in Campbell River for the weekend. This was home base for the crew. Just after lunch and clean-up, Anna went up to the top deck to sit in the sun and watch as they pulled into the harbour. It was the first break she'd had all week and she felt the exhaustion seep out of her as the warm noon sun bathed her face and arms.

"Hey! What do you think this is? A fuckin' cruise ship?" It was Red again.

"But I'm all done down there," Anna replied.

"Yeah, well, get down there and find something to do, Cookie. No one slacks off on my boat until the prow kisses the dock."

During the half hour before they negotiated their way to their mooring, Anna seethed in the hot galley. Some of the guys came in and demanded beers, talking non-stop about what and where they would drink and *what* they'd fuck while they were in town.

"Hey Red, didja ever bone that dumb blonde that was hangin' around last time we were in?" Buck said, shoving his big index finger in and out of the opening in his fist in a crude gesture.

"Yeah, I dogged her. Fuck, she was a dumb cunt."

"Well, ya don't want 'em with too much brains. It's the dumb ones give good head."

"Har-har-har," in chorus.

"What about her fat little friend, Ed? You gonna get her this weekend? She's always hanging around the

Schooner looking like she'd pay for it. Yer wife can't be puttin' out much these days. No offense, but she looks like a beached whale. When she gonna pop that kid anyway?"

"Fuck off, Hog. You look like you could pop a kid yourself any minute," Ed retorted, slapping Hog's enormous gut.

"Har-har-har," in chorus.

"Seriously man, when's the kid due?" Hog asked.

"Any day now, and I hope she doesn't do it while I'm in town. She wants me to fuckin' be there and there's no fuckin' way, man. I can't handle all that blood'n shit." Ed looked grim.

"So, ya gonna get some tail while ya can, Ed? That fat little thing wants you for sure," said the one they called Sharkey, giving Ed a jocular poke in the ribs. Apparently Sharkey was this guy's actual last name; it was disturbing how well it suited him. He was all sinewy and sleek-looking, with slits for eyes, and he had a way of sliding quietly around and standing too close.

"Fuck off, Sharkey. You guys are a bunch of pigs. Can't you see there's a lady present?" Ed gestured mockingly toward Anna.

"Har-har-har," in chorus.

Anna ignored them as she sat staring out the galley porthole. *As soon as the boat docks these jerks leave and go drink their faces off and I'll be left in peace,* she told herself. She planned to stretch out in the sun for the rest of the day and curl up with her book that evening. She was reading a Marilyn French novel that she'd borrowed from the women's centre at the college.

"Hey Cookie, ya gonna come out for a beer with us?" Big Red asked solicitously.

"Yeah Cookie, come on out and be sociable. We'll buy ya a couple of beers," Buck offered.

"No thanks. I think I'll just stay here—but thanks."

"Don't worry, babe, we'll protect you from all the animals out there," Sharkey said with a toothy grin.

"No, really, it's OK. I'd rather just stay here. I'm pretty tired."

"Oh yeah, right, it must be all that hard work you been doin', eh?" Big Red quipped. "C'mon, guys, let's leave the princess here. I've got a boner that can't wait."

"Har-har-har," in chorus.

To Anna's relief they finally gave up and started filing out of the stuffy room. In a few minutes they had secured the boat, then they were gone.

The rest of the day was blissfully quiet. Anna sat up on the top deck letting the gentle rocking of the boat and the seagulls' cries overhead take her to another world. She imagined she was on her own sailboat anchored out in some lovely tropical bay. At sundown she went inside, made herself a sandwich and opened her book.

The crew was hung over the next day as they readied the boat for the trip out that evening. Their breath was foul and every few minutes one of them would break wind and make some grade-school joke about it. The predictable har-har-hars grated on Anna more than usual.

Just one more week, she told herself as she went into town to shop for groceries. I'll stick it out just one more week and if it doesn't get any better, I'll quit. She called her cousin collect and talked to her little boy. She felt like shit when he started to cry.

Anna had no idea how much money they'd made that week; the guys weren't talking. If the salmon were running and the next week was a good one she knew she could walk away with up to five grand and that would do it. It would have to.

That evening, they headed up the coast toward the Queen Charlotte Islands and after travelling all night, the boat pulled in briefly at Bella Bella for fuel. They maintained full speed all that day in calm seas. To Anna's delight, porpoise played off the prow of the ship for hours. The porpoise were taking turns surfing on the swell created by the force of the prow cutting through the water. The same way seagulls catch the air currents, Anna supposed. If she leaned over the rail and dangled her arm, she could almost touch them. One of the creatures actually rolled over on its side and watched her with one large intelligent eye. Anna checked to see if she was alone up front and seeing that she was, began singing softly to it. "Beautiful, beautiful brown eyes…"

She was startled when she heard Big Red's voice.

"Hey, Cookie, quit singin' to the fish and get to work." Anna was mortified. She could feel the heat creep up her face and she knew her cheeks were red. God, he never lets up! It's as though he follows me around just looking for some way to humiliate me. Shit, that guy pisses me off. Reluctantly, she went back down to the galley to look busy until it was time to start dinner. She had few breaks from the stifling heat of the galley and she longed to be outside in the fresh air. When she had offered to help on deck, the crew just laughed. "Go bake a cake. This is man's work," they sneered.

The next day, the *Coho Queen* was anchored along with a gaggle of other fish boats waiting their turn to do a set, when news of a large pod of killer whales moving their way came over the ship's radio. Within an hour the boat was surrounded by more than a dozen of the creatures. Orca, the native Indian people called them. The name, like the giant sea mammals themselves, had a magical quality for Anna.

Anna began to notice that everything wasn't quite right on board. The guys were storming around the deck cursing and kicking stuff over. Two of the guys almost got into a fist-fight. They were all drinking more than usual for a working day. Anna finally decided to ask what was going on. Buck came through the galley from the engine room after cutting the engine.

"What's up, Buck? Why's everyone so pissed off?" she asked tentatively.

"The fuckin' blackfish are eatin' up all our fuckin' salmon is what's up," he snarled. "And we have to just sit here and watch until they're finished. Goddam greedy bastards. I'd shoot every goddam one of 'em if I had my way."

"But surely there are enough salmon down there to feed the whales and still net some?" Anna knew the killer whales were indigenous to the coastal waters of British Columbia and she'd never heard of a shortage of salmon.

"You really are a dumb broad, aren't you? Don't you know dick about nothin'? The whales are here because they know there's a salmon run here—same reason we're here, you see." He was talking to Anna as though she were six years old. "So they come and spend a couple of hours eating about a half-ton of sockeye each and the rest, they chase up to Alaska. Meanwhile we can't put out our nets because they just swim right through them and rip the shit outa them. Could even pull the boat down if one got caught up an' decided to dive. There, you've had your little fishing lesson. Now get outa my way or I'll throw you overboard and you can see for yourself what's going on down there."

He pushed past her roughly, knocking her painfully into the doorway before she had a chance to respond.

Anna choked down her rage and sneaked up to the

top deck where she hunkered down in a corner to watch. Magnificent backs and dorsal fins were cresting the water all around the boat, some of them within twenty feet of where she sat. A little further out she could see smaller glossy fins of young orca break the surface close beside what must be their mothers. In awe, Anna felt deep in her soul that she was privileged to witness these wild beings in their element. She could feel their spirits all around her. They weren't just fish to Anna. *They* have a right to be here, she thought. It was the gathering of seiners and trollers that was alien, sitting like unwieldy lumps on the surface of the orca world.

Anna felt sick when she overheard the crew talking about how they and many other fishermen had gone out and shot the whales, until a law was passed preventing it. She decided that men who did this really must be a different species. One that raped and beat women and children and killed beautiful wild creatures without a thought. Well, Anna thought, if there is a God, these men will all end up in hell. Wherever they did end up, Anna prayed that they wouldn't be in the same afterworld as hers.

Near the end of the week, the killer whales moved on and the crew could finally put the net out. In their first set, along with a pitifully small number of sockeye, a handful of coho and a variety of other fish Anna didn't recognize, they netted a four-and-a-half foot dogfish which tore up the net badly before they got it up on deck. Dogfish, or mudsharks as they were also called, looked just like small sharks. And this one's none too small, thought Anna. The guys seemed to take a perverse pleasure in killing the dogfish before they tossed it overboard. Anna didn't exactly feel sorry for the dogfish—it was a cold and sinister-looking thing—but to watch the crew go at it with such brutality and enthusiasm...It gives me the creeps, she thought. It's like watching evil kill evil. After a while she couldn't watch.

Anna was looking forward to the weekend. The *Coho Queen* was docking at Steveston so the crew could repair the net. The trip back in the cold and rain was mostly uneventful. A choppy sea made it hard for Anna to keep her food down, but she used the anti-nausea pills she'd bought in Bella Bella and she got through it without throwing up. As she was cleaning up and checking supplies the morning they arrived in Steveston, the skipper called her up on deck.

"Hey Cookie, come here."

"What do you want, Red?" Anna was annoyed. She just wanted to finish up and leave.

"I said, come here, and when your skipper gives an order you don't ask why."

Arrogant bastard, she thought, but she stepped out on deck and looked around. He was on the upper deck looking down at her with a smart-ass expression on his face. He tossed his head in that way some men have of summoning their women. The boys at school used to do that at dances when they wanted to ask her to dance. Anna used to think it was sexy. At this moment she felt like decapitating him. She climbed the ladder to the upper deck and followed Big Red to the skipper's cabin at the front of the boat. He stopped at the door.

"What do you want, Red? I'm busy and I want to get going."

"Come in," he said, gesturing past himself into the cramped quarters. Anna could see the radio equipment and his bunk just over his shoulder. A voice in her head said, *Don't do it*, but then it occurred to her that he may just want to show her something about the radio or perhaps there was some contract she needed to sign, since she hadn't been asked to do that yet. Against her better instincts, Anna stepped over the sill past him and into the cabin.

"Take your clothes off and get into bed." He indicated the filthy bunk with that same toss of his head.

Anna couldn't believe her ears. You prick, she thought. You ugly, arrogant prick! How dare you!

"No," she said flatly.

"Do as you're told or you're fired. It's that simple," he said with a smug smile that was more like a slit in his beefy face.

"No thanks, Red. The thought of sleeping with you makes my stomach turn." Anna edged toward the open doorway. The hair was going up at the back of her neck, sending goosebumps down her arms.

His arm shot out to close the sliding door but it stuck for a moment. In that moment, Anna was out.

"You cunt," he spat as he lunged at her. His hand caught the back of her T-shirt but she twisted free and saw him lurch off balance as she turned the corner at a run.

As Anna bolted down the ladder two rungs at a time, fear slammed into her like a fist in her belly and she couldn't breathe. She ducked into the galley and grabbed her knapsack. She could hear Red coming down the ladder—didn't know if she could make it out the door and off the boat in time. She glanced at the open doorway, her thoughts darting around like trapped sparrows.

I know what he'll do to me if he catches me, she thought. As that image formed, anger—like a strong cold wind—flooded her body. With precision and clarity, Anna measured the distance she would have to cover. Her first leap took her to the sill of the galley door, the second to mid-deck, and with the third leap she placed both hands on the ship's side-rail and vaulted over it onto the dock. She landed in a squat and, adjusting her knapsack, she headed up the wharf at a run.

"Not worth the trouble—bitch!" she heard Red yell as she ran.

Anna was breathing hard when she reached the pay phone. As she paused to catch her breath, she was overcome with dizziness. She opened and closed her eyes, afraid that she would black out. She couldn't rid herself of the sensation that the ground beneath her was tipping precariously from side to side. Instinctively, she stretched out both her arms to counter the vertigo. A moment later, Anna realized she must still have her "sea legs." She still felt the need to steady herself with a hand on the side of the phone booth as she dug into her pocket for change to call a cab.

Anna had been home for two days when Big Red called to let her know that he'd meant it when he'd said she was fired and that her cheque was in the mail. She still didn't know how much money she'd made. She wondered if any amount was worth what she'd had to put up with.

"So, Red, what is your actual reason for firing me?" she inquired.

"You were a shitty cook," he sneered and hung up.

"Lying coward," Anna said as she slammed the receiver down. "I hope you fall overboard and drown."

The small paycheque she received in the mail the next day made her wish it even more fervently. She knew there was no point in going after him for it. She had no contract and it would be their word against hers. Five to one.

Over the next few weeks, it slowly dawned on Anna

that if she hadn't managed to escape when she did, Big Red would have raped her without a second thought. Every time she thought about him she felt a stab of fear and the slow burn of her rage.

Four years after Anna's experience on the *Coho Queen*, she received a phone call from her former boyfriend.

"Hey, you remember the skipper on the *Coho Queen* that you worked for that summer?"

"Yeah, hard guy to forget. What about him?"

"Last week they found him floating face down with his fly open."

Har-har-har, Anna thought to herself.

Dolls and Teddies

For Bunky

I RESCUE DOLLS AND TEDDIES. I rescue them from the Goodwill, garage sales, and flea markets. I take them home, abandoned waifs. They call out to me from their boxes and shelves. Their arms poke out hopefully toward me. Sometimes their legs, sticking desperately out, crammed upside down among hard trucks and guns and other toys, attract my attention. I *know* they can't breathe.

At first I intend only to turn them right side up, give them some air. Then their little button eyes lock with mine. Vacant and soulless. Black holes to fall and fall into.

Other people pass by indifferently. Only *I* can hear the pathetic voices, the desolate whimpers of these little orphans. Only *I* can see the furtive gestures, the hopeless attempts to rub dirt off a cheek or run a stiff hand through knotted hair. If one eye is missing, the other looks at me with twice the longing. Only *I* can feel their little dolly feelings, their tiny hearts thumping in their little teddy tummies. I know it is up to me.

So home we go. I tuck them under my arm or inside my pockets. Right side up always. No bags. No scary darkness. Close to my heart. I can feel their gratitude; it clutches at me with desperate little claws.

They've caught my eye, captured my heart. They are saved, rescued; I am captured, caught.

Once home, a gentle warm bath, maybe some kitchy-coos. I try to elicit some smiles or giggles but they are often too forlorn, not yet sure enough of me. I'm careful not to get soap in their eyes, not to immerse their heads. I keep a firm grip always. After towel drying, I begin gentle tugging at hair or fur with a comb. They have hopeless straggles and clumps and bald patches, especially the dolls with rows of holes in their naked rubber heads. I kiss the bald spots and carry on. When we've done the best we can it's out to the sun to sit and dry. A healing time. On a rainy day I use the blow dryer with a prelude of reassuring words. Before I stitch a tear, mend a wound, reset an eye, I use hypnosis. For the pain.

There—whole and dry, dressed or swaddled securely in something soft and clean. Now the namings can begin.

I do not presume to name them myself. I don't just pull a name out of the universe and stick it on, impose it. I ask. Then I wait. The dolls and teddies know their own names, of course, and will give them willingly in exchange for love.

That is how Angus Ransterd George-Me-Bear came into being, also Punchy Bunky Bear-Person and Nancy and Sleeping Beauty.

I, myself, am still waiting, stiff-legged, arms outstretched hopefully, to come into being. Perhaps someone will see me today.

I have changed. I have changed my name, changed diapers, changed my mind, changed the expression on my face, changed clothes...I have changed my emotional posture in order to receive or defend what is thrown at me in life.

Who I am does not change. I am the aftermath of my own childhood and I still cower at a raised fist or a showing of teeth or the absence of love promised forever.

MORE FICTION FROM POLESTAR PRESS:

Alaska Highway Two-Step, Caroline Woodward • $12.95

Bloodsong and Other Stories of South Africa, Ernst Havemann • $9.95

Disturbing The Peace, Caroline Woodward • $12.95

Imperfect Moments, Candis Graham • $14.95

The Magpie Summer, Judith Wright • $9.95

Mobile Homes, Noel Hudson • $9.95

Rapid Transits and Other Stories, Holley Rubinsky • $12.95

The Rocket, The Flower, The Hammer, and Me: An All-Star Collection of Canadian Hockey Fiction, Doug Beardsley, editor • $9.95

Sitting In The Club Car Drinking Rum and Karma-Kola: A Manual of Etiquette for Ladies Crossing Canada By Train, Paulette Jiles • $10.95

Song To The Rising Sun: A Collection, Paulette Jiles • $12.95

Tasmanian Tiger, Jane Barker Wright • $12.95

Vancouver Fiction, David Watmough, editor • $12.95

POETRY FROM POLESTAR PRESS:

Being On The Moon, Annharte • $10.95

Bewildered Rituals, Sandy Shreve • $12.95

Covering Rough Ground, Kate Braid • $11.95

Jesse James Poems, Paulette Jiles • $10.95

A Labour Of Love: An Anthology of Poetry on Pregnancy and Child-birth, Mona Fertig, editor • $12.95

no visual scars, Angela Hryniuk • $12.95

North Book, Jim Green • $7.95

On The Way To Ethiopia, Allan Safarik • $11.95

Queen Of All The Dustballs and Other Epics of Everyday Life, Bill Richardson • $14.95

The Gathering: Stones For The Medicine Wheel, Gregory Scofield • $12.95

Vancouver Poetry, Allan Safarik, editor • $12.95

The Weight Of My Raggedy Skin, Dale Zieroth • $11.95

Whylah Falls, George Elliott Clarke • $12.95

X-Ray Of Longing, Glen Downie • $9.95